In the Shadow of Monte Bianco

Book II in the Inferos Vortex Series

by

G. Filotto

ISBN 978-1-8381586-2-0

A Ca' Filo Imprint

***

This is a work of fiction. All characters, organisations, and events portrayed in this novel are either products of the author's imagination or are used fictitiously.

Dedication
To my wife Lucie and all our children.
You know who you are.

To the children

I'm not putting all of your names down because even though this is book 2 of the series, I am still not sure when your mother will decide we have had enough brothers and sisters for you all, but to be clear this dedication includes any of you born after I wrote this one too.

A Note to the Reader

This is the second book in the Inferos Vortex Series. In order to understand the setting, it is highly advisable the first book in the series is read first. The book's title is:

In the Shadow of Monte Castello

This can be purchased cheaper in digital format either at G. Filotto's E-book store here:

https://payhip.com/EBOOKSBYGFILOTTO

or in paperback format at Amazon.com, where his author's page can be found here:

https://www.amazon.com/stores/Giuseppe%20Filotto/author/B0051VGAAM

If you enjoy this book, please be kind enough to leave a positive review so others may benefit too. Thank you.

1

Douglas Jones stood next to his assistant Cooper Chauvin, who had a live frog in a medium sized jar in his hands, and wore thick welder's gloves. As if the harmless amphibian in the jar was a dangerous combination of radioactive nitro-glycerine, that might explode at any second, the expression on Cooper's face was a mixture of intense focus and existential worry, as he began to open the jar, carefully leaning it towards the recently deceased red dragon lying on the field before him. The sulphurous smell emanating from the creature's still thinly smoking nostrils made the seemingly absurd situation very real to all present, in case the large creature's dead body wasn't enough.

Taro Valenti, and his nine-year old son Marco, also stood close to the dead dragon. The rest of his family, stood a little behind them. Jane, his wife, blue eyed and with dark hair loose and down to the middle of her back, had a semi-automatic Ruger SFAR in .308 slung on her shoulder. She had not had time to tie up her hair when the children all wanted to run out and see the dragon that Taro, with help from Marco, had shot down a scant half hour earlier. Anna, his eldest daughter at fifteen, carried a sleek hunting rifle in 7mm Remington, with a good scope on it, and a .38 special revolver on an outside the belt holster, on her right hip. Scarlet, now eleven, had learnt to be safer with firearms over the last three years, but she preferred a semi-automatic Ruger in .22 LR with the special silver bullets loaded with a drop of Holy Water. Taro always felt she was not having enough gun with her, but Scarlet had shown she was scarily accurate with that pistol. Arianna at age 8 was still a little young to be trusted with a loaded gun at all times, but on this occasion, she had her dad's small PPK in a shoulder holster, which made her feel like a very cool secret agent, and she had dubbed herself Arianna Danger. Alina, the five-year old simply held her mom's hand and watched silently and curiously, before asking from behind her father:

"Daddy?"

"Yes darling?" Said Taro without turning around.

"Daddy, what is the long man doing with the frog?"

Taro smiled. Cooper was fairly tall after all.

"He's going to put the frog on the dead dragon to see if it's safe."

"But why a frog, daddy?"

"Our friend Douglas has been doing experiments, and frogs are the most sensitive to any bad stuff these creatures that come through the portals may produce. Some are really bad, like the Hellfrog. But luckily only very few of those have ever come through, and apparently they can't reproduce on this plane. Which is a good thing, given what Douglas has told us about them."

"That's the one that killed his friend. The Hellfrog."

"Yes darling. It is. But now let's just be quiet a bit, okay?"

Taro knew Douglas still felt bad about his original assistant dying when he had reached out to touch the very first creature that had been ported in years ago, by his experiment. And he felt partly responsible for all the other 666 portals that had been opened three years ago. Douglas had shut down those portals, but now there were a handful more; a six-fingered hand at that. One on each continent except Antarctica; and Douglas knew this dragon was from one of those portals. Dragons had not been seen before today as far as he knew, and he was one of a very few people that would receive notifications of sightings of new creatures before most of the rest of the planet, or what was left of it.

The whole scene before them was both surreal and yet also extremely tangible and present. Taro noticed the large red scales on the back of the dragon, becoming smaller and turning to a paler yellowish colour on the underbelly. The large leathery wings, one folded badly under the large body of it, the other half opened still, part of its membrane lazily being moved about by the slight breeze. And the dark blood oozing from the wounds Taro and Marco had inflicted on the creature by shooting it. It was all very real, as was the smell of burnt grass. The olive tree that had caught fire when the dragon had flailed its head aside due to the buckshot Taro had fired into its snout and face, was still smouldering a few dozen metres away. The grass near the dragon's head was singed, with a smell reminiscent of gunsmoke tinged with acrid sulphur rising from the thing's still slightly smoking mouth and nostrils. Its mouth half-opened, the lower jaw broken by Marco's rifle round, had crocodile-like teeth, though much larger than any crocodile Taro had ever seen.

Cooper leaned the opened jar over the dead dragon and the frog hopped out of it, landing on the dragon. It sat there a few seconds, then hopped on, across the dragon's back with its red scales, and eventually off it on the far side after a few jumps.

"Let it go," said Douglas. "He's earned his freedom."

Cooper looked relieved, but he spoke nevertheless, "We still have to test its soft tissues, saliva, blood…"

"And you will, but that frog should be set free now."

"Fair enough," replied Cooper.

"Dad, can I get my dragon skin for the jacket now? Can I skin it?" asked Marco excitedly. After he had shot the beast, Marco had told his father he wanted to make a jacket out of the dragon skin.

Taro laughed.

"Sure son, but let Cooper check it's safe first. It will take a while. And I think you'll need some help skinning the thing, it's pretty big."

"I want a jacket too!" said Arianna predictably. She was closest to Marco in age, and always wanted to do whatever he was up to.

"You need to shoot your own dragon then!" said Marco.

"Daa-ddyyy… Marco is being mean to me!"

Taro turned his head to look at both Marco next to him and Arianna slightly behind him. They both knew the dad look, which in recent years, due to the extreme circumstances of there being werewolves, vampires, and various other dangerous critters still about from time to time, had achieved a new meaning; resulting in both Marco and Arianna's immediate silence; due to what Taro insisted to Jane was correct fatherly respect, but she insisted was mostly fear of an arse whooping from dad. "Tomato-Tomatoe," would reply Taro.

Having spent decades training men in martial arts in previous decades, Taro had a very clear sense of what humans required to attain focus, discipline, a quick mind, and good reactions.

They were all more necessary than ever, given that some four billion people had been killed by the various monstrosities that had come out from the portals of three years ago, and not all of the demonic spawn were destroyed yet.

The occasional kick in the butt for not listening and executing with sufficient speed and precision whatever dad said, was a small price to pay to ensure his children had a better chance at surviving whatever the future of this fantastic new world would bring. Case in point, Marco had probably saved his life by taking the decision to reload his rifle and start firing at the dragon, instead of staying in hiding behind the tree as his father had told him to do. As Taro had run up to the wounded dragon to shoot it at close range in order to finish it off, it had turned, and might well have cooked him with a blast of its fiery breath if Marco had not been shooting at it too.

Both Marco and Arianna went silent, then Marco, looking at his father a little longer said in a soft voice:

"Okay Arianna, I'll help you pick out some dragon skin for a jacket too then."

Anna and Scarlet barely glanced at each other before saying in unison: "Can we have one too dad?"

"Ask your brother, it's his skin," replied Taro wanting to avoid the drama that was sure to follow.

Marco looked at Taro meaningfully, "Dad… is it really my skin?"

"Yes son. You decide who gets what."

Marco looked at his father in silence for a bit then nodded. He knew it was a kind of test, and he meant to pass it.

Jane unexpectedly spoke up next, in her British accented English.

"But Marco, you will save a good piece for mommy too, right, so we can all look cool with your dragon skin jacket idea."

There she goes with the usual emotional blackmail! Thought Taro, but he was not worried. Marco had four sisters, which meant he was essentially immune to emotional manipulation by now.

"Okay mommy. You can have a jacket. But you're going to sew mine first."

Taro laughed. Jane had had some of his work clothes to patch for the last four years, since before the portals, and she had not used her sewing machine on any of them yet.

"Smart boy, Marco!" said his father.

The dragon was huge, about ten or eleven metres from head to tip of the tail, the tail being about half of the total length. It's wing span was at least as wide as it was long. And yet, Taro had the impression this was probably a younger dragon, not an ancient and really big one. He had told Douglas he wondered if perhaps the things that came through the portals were an amalgam of the thoughts and ideas of the supernatural that humans had had throughout the ages. And given that the game of Dungeons and Dragons, and hundreds of variations of the theme had been played by literally millions of teenagers when Taro was young, before personal computers existed, he had expressed the thought to Douglas that maybe at least in part some of the beings coming through were realised thought-forms from a nightmare dimension. It was a hypothesis anyway. And as good as any other that had been presented so far. And a red dragon that fit pretty precisely what he and so many other teenagers had imagined they might look like, some four decades earlier, made Taro think his theory had more than a little merit.

"Was it alone?" asked Douglas.

"We didn't see any others, but for all I know this is an advance scout," replied Taro.

"Right," said Douglas concerned. Then he added:

"I'm going to get the base in Rimini to send a couple of those Humvees with .50 cals over, and tell them to get their anti-aircraft weapons out of storage and in working order. There's not been much use for shooting at things in the air until now."

"Good idea Douglas. I hate to think they could just come at night and set fire to our houses."

"Well, you have the safe rooms and the bunker, so you'd be fine, but yes, it would be a nuisance. Maybe sleep in the bunker tonight? I and Kate and the kids will, at our place."

Taro nodded.

"Alright Doug. I'm going to get some lunch, along with the tribe. You want to stay and eat with us?"

"I better get back, let Kate know what's going on."

"Radio her to come over with the kids. I made plenty," said Jane as they started back up the hill, leaving Cooper to run his tests, as he opened what looked like a small leather suitcase similar to a larger version of what a doctor from the 1800s would have used.

"Cooper, you come eat something too when you're done," said Jane, always careful to include everyone, as her polite English nature required.

"Thank you Mrs. Valenti, I will," said Cooper gratefully, He had not had breakfast this morning and he was hungry.

"Don't make me feel old Cooper, it's Jane."

"Sorry Mrs… Jane…"

Jane smiled as she turned back towards the house. Her hair lose it caught in the breeze a little as she walked a short way ahead of Taro, Douglas and some of the children. Alina had taken hold of Taro's hand and was walking quietly next to him. She usually wanted to be near her father more than most of the other children, though she was the only one with her mother's blue eyes. A recessive gene Taro too had from his own mother, although his eyes were green. Alina's blonde hair was still light, unlike Marco's that had started to get darker now, as Taro's own had from childhood towards approaching puberty.

Taro noticed that he wasn't the only one appreciating his wife's shapely behind as they walked back towards the house. Douglas had noted it too, but not lecherously. The man simply had eyes in his head, one could hardly blame him. Besides, Douglas' own wife was attractive too. Neither man had any even mildly improper thoughts towards the other's spouse, both simply had a similar appreciation of life as it happened around them.

Taro also noted that it was a sunny, good day, not too warm nor windy. And his children were all smart and good looking. And he was alive and not a crispy dragon snack. *Always a bonus!* He thought to himself, and his wife had a very pretty arse despite being in her fourth decade now. Life was good, and he thanked God for it all. *Especially for her pretty arse too, Lord. You know I don't mean any disrespect by it. I really like that pretty behind of hers. Thanks again.*

He was fairly sure his priest would not approve of such prayers. Too close to the way Pagan Romans or Greeks might have spoken to their "gods". Which in Catholic thought were the Watchers that had failed miserably to follow God's instructions to teach and lead mankind, and had been punished for it, as Psalm 81 of Catholic Bibles told. Reflecting on the idea that speaking to essentially selfish and evil spirits like a man talking to, if not an equal at least someone he did not necessarily have deep reverence for, was not how one should address Jesus Christ the Son, nor God the Father, he corrected himself internally.

Sorry Lord. I'll try to be better. But you did make her pretty, and surely appreciating beauty is a good thing. After all, look at how many children your pretty creation has blessed me with. Thank you, Lord.

Eh, he thought, *probably not much of an improvement.* But then that blue sundress did cling to her as she walked in the breeze, and Taro was enjoying the rush of life that one gets when you narrowly survive something dangerous yet exciting. And few things got more exciting that shooting down a red dragon with your nine-year old boy.

2

The Valenti and Jones families and Cooper Chauvin had all had lunch together while some of the farmhands had started skinning the dragon, alongside a few armed guards. Marco had left the table early as he wanted to help with the skinning, and Arianna had gone with him, though only to watch, or so she had said, but Taro knew she was one of the least squeamish kids he had known, except when it came to insects for some reason. The Chinese stink bugs that had infested Italy for the last twenty years or so were her nemesis. Harmless except for the stink they produced if you molested them, they were quite large and noisy when they flew, and she still acted as if they were poisonous flying rats whenever one came close to her.

Cooper had brought out the latest version of his Monster Compendium that he had been adding to as soon as a new species of creature that had come through the portals was discovered. It was a loving creation, updated regularly and it included pictures, photographs and detailed information on each creature, a true encyclopaedia of the things that had come through the portals. He had added the preliminary information on the red dragon entry using his ruggerised, military issue, portable laptop, which he had extracted from his field kit in the leather case, even as they sat at the table. And he had then forwarded a copy to the Valenti, using their local intranet in the house.

Taro had glanced at the index, noting the titles of the various entries. It formed an alphabetical list that was both impressive and worrying.

Ant, Giant	*Carnivorous Plants, Various*
Ape, Giant	*Centipede, Giant*
Bee, Giant	*Chimera*
Beetle, Giant	*Cockatrice*

Crab, Giant

Crocodile, Giant

Dinosaur (?), Various

Doppelganger (rare?), Dangerous

Dragon, Red

Facehugger

Faerie, Various

Gargoyle, Various

Ghoul

Ghost/Phantom/Poltergeist/Spirit

Gibbering Mouther

Gnoll

Goblin

Gorgon

Gray Ooze

Griffon

Hag/Lich/Revenant/Wight/Wraith

Harpy

Hellboar

Hellfrog

Hellhound

Insect Swarm, Various

Imp/Homunculus, Various

Leech, Giant

Lizard, Giant, Various

Lycanthrope, Wolf

Lycanthrope, Bear

Lycanthrope, Rat

Lycanthrope, Devil Swine

Manticore

Minotaur

Mosquito, Giant

Mujina

Orc

Porcupine, Giant

Scorpion, Giant

Shapeshifter

Shark, Giant

Slug, Giant

Snail, Giant

Snake, Giant, Various

Spider, Giant, Various

Stirge

Toad, Giant

Undead/Zombie

Vampire

Wasp, Giant

Worm, Giant

"Cooper, where did you get these names from?" asked Taro. He had noticed that, on this latest version, many of the names had been updated from the ones he had seen a few months previous.

"I found a copy of a Dungeons and Dragons Cyclopedia at the army base in Rimini. Some of the guys had played it and they were always talking about it, and how we were now living in a mix of our world and the D&D world, and on reading it, well… I thought it made sense to change some of the names."

"So… I'm not the only one that thinks some of these things could be related to our thoughts about them. Some of these monster types are pretty unique to the D&D realm, after all, like this Gibbering Mouther…"

"Well," said Cooper a little sheepishly, "That's just what I called it after Douglas gave me a description of that nightmare vision he had when he touched that black rock, before it exploded."

"So, there hasn't been one seen other than in Douglas' vision?"

"Not that we know of. I explained it in the description…" trailed off Cooper. Taro just nodded as he continued to study the index.

"What about Orcs?"

"Well, again, it's just my best guess and approximation based on what the recovered bodies or photographs look like, and the descriptions we get. And some things have no equivalent in the monster manuals of Dungeons and Dragons, like the Hellfrog."

"Yeah…" replied Taro, thinking, *probably because it would have been thought of as an unfair monster created by a sadistic Dungeon Master that wanted to just kill his players for fun.* But he didn't say anything, out of respect for Douglas' sensitivity to Hellfrogs.

"Anyway, Cooper, thanks for the update. I have some reading to do," said Taro as he closed the iPad's screen cover.

That evening, both the Valenti and Jones families slept in their respective home bunkers. Taro stayed up late into the night reading up on the descriptions and scrutinising the photographs and even videos embedded under each monster entry. Cooper's Monster Compendium was soon shortened to Cooper's Compendium in his mind, which made him smile, as it sounded like an expansion set volume for Dungeons and Dragons, despite the far from entertaining entries, some of which were terrifying and gruesome.

He resolved to make sure he didn't tell Jane about the disembodied or invisible ghosts/spirits or whatever they were. She was terrified by the idea of ghosts even *before* they became a real thing. It might be best if she didn't become a drooling wreck at the thought of them, now that they were actually a thing. Especially since the protection against them was scant, and mostly had to do with circling the area with salt and holy water. Both of which things Taro had already done, since they quickly took all the required precautions as soon as Douglas sent out his weekly newsletter, which usually made its way around the world in short order. Luckily the ghost things were rare and most people thought they had been dispatched by spraying holy water that had the smoke of frankincense bubbled through it. This had been discovered by a group in France that had managed to trap one of these invisible entities in a metal vault within a bank. They had placed a holy water imbibed sheet over the opening and apparently the spirit could not phase through steel or the sheet. They had tested various weapons against it until someone had thought of the weird idea of bubbling frankincense through holy water and then spraying the thing with it. It could be seen on infrared cameras apparently, as a cold spot, and it retained a more or less humanoid shape, until it was disintegrated by the holy water concoction.

Reading about the spirit/ghost thing had not worried Taro unduly, he had always had a natural faith that he was more powerful than incorporeal spirits, but the entry on the Doppelganger and its seemingly related cousins the Mujina and the Shapeshifters, made the hair on the back of his neck stand on end. One had apparently lived with a family for a year, pretending to be the uncle, before it killed and ate their children one night. There seemed to be almost no way of spotting them other than by intimate knowledge of the people you knew and noting any strange behaviour. Not the easiest thing to do in a world that had been overrun with supernatural and evil creatures from a dimension Taro was sure was Hell itself.

They already had the rule to never be alone outside the house, but he promised himself to remind everyone of how important it was. He would mention the Doppelganger, without getting into the gory and horrifying specifics that made sleep impossible for him for the rest of the night.

3

Douglas had not slept at all either. He had been in communication with both the HAARP facilities in Alaska and DARPA, and confirmed that once again, the portals had all appeared as a result of activity at the CERN supercollider.

The volume of activity at each portal was higher than a dozen of the older and smaller portals had been. He also tested and realised that using the HAARP inducers alone would not do it. Calculating the energy requirements, he realised that nothing short of a nuclear strike directly on the vortex, and then only with the HAARP modulated frequency of the scalar resonances precisely fixed about a second or two before impact could it possibly disrupt the portal. Always assuming it didn't rip it open more.

The portal in North America was causing massive issues. It had been centred on a Canadian town called Regina, not too far North of the American border and the creatures pouring out of it were so numerous and dangerous that the American command simply launched four ICBMs at it with nuclear warheads and got the HAARP station in Alaska to modulate the frequency as per the calculations Douglas had sent them. They had not told him they intended to do this, and Douglas was unaware it had been done until on his screen he saw the portal in North America flare up enormously, almost like a scalar mini Nova explosion, the scalar shockwave had a diameter of three thousand miles.

It was an hour before he heard back from the US mainland. They had closed the portal but the shock wave had also released a bunch of creatures that had apparently materialised spontaneously within the radius of the scalar Nova-effect. There were early reports of some of the creatures materialising partially embedded in walls, vehicles, the Earth itself, and most horrific of all, within some very unlucky human beings. There was no estimate of the death-toll yet, but Douglas estimated it must be in the tens of thousands at least, and possibly in the hundreds of thousands if not millions by the time the newly ported fiends had done their jobs.

It had been 1:11 am when the North American detonation and portal shut down had taken place. The Portal in Asia was towards the South East, of China, close to the more populous areas. And the Chinese military had already taken heavy losses three years ago. They were busy evacuating people with the brutality and efficiency only China could muster. They had asked for 24 hours to get as many people out of the blast zone as possible, while Russian nuclear warheads were being prepared aboard Russian long-distance bombers for deployment.

Australia had no easy answer as none of the nuclear ICBMs that were still operational were in range. It may well end up being a lost continent, thought Douglas.

The African vortex was in Chad and, once again, out of reach of nuclear warheads, after all, who would want to nuke Chad? Nevertheless, an American aircraft carrier that had been left in the Mediterranean was en-route, and in a few days could launch. It was simply assumed that Chad would be nuked. It wasn't even going to be discussed, partly because there was no way to get in touch with many parts of Africa yet, aside Southern Africa, and even then, the communications were scant. That left the South American portal, which was at the tip of Chile, in the previously inappropriately named *Tierra del Fuego*, given how cold it was. And today it might even be literally on fire, for all Douglas knew. There wasn't much going on there, and no contact. Once again, American aircraft carriers had to be dispatched to the area.

And finally, there was the European one. Near Mt. Blanc. Or Monte Bianco as they called it in Italy. Over 500 kilometres from where Doug was now, but nuking that area would wipe out too much of Europe, especially given the subsequent three-thousand-mile diameter shockwave, not to mention the actual atomic explosions.

Douglas spent the rest of the night trying to think of alternative solutions for the European portal. And how to convince the Americans, or the Russians, or anyone really, to nuke the crap out of CERN, and Davos. But he knew Switzerland was the most nuclear fortified country on Earth, with literal underground cities, designed to lack for nothing, and a bunker in every home that doubled as a cellar.

All I wanted to do was bring humanity to the stars, thought Douglas dejectedly. *I didn't mean for all of this, Lord, forgive me.*

His wife Kate knew what was going through her husband's head and called him to bed in the early morning.

"Babe, you didn't do this. Remember that you had told them to shut it down."

It was true, Douglas had tried to stop any further work on the portals once the Hellfrog incident, and he personally had stopped working on that issue, but others did not. He still felt responsible. It made it very hard to sleep with the shadow of some four billion souls having been lost to the 666 portals that had been opened by the CERN lab in some way, three years previous. Douglas had personally overseen the shutting down of almost every one of those portals over a period of a few days. He'd been going on rage, guilt, and some stimulants the army had, and had basically gone almost a week without sleep. Kate had no intention of seeing him do that to himself again.

"Listen, you know this stuff better than anyone alive. You will figure it out. There has to be another way. You will find it. Now come to bed." She kissed him, and slowly, he relented. She knew how to see to it her husband would sleep —at least for a few hours— the sleep of the just.

4

The US Air Force base at Aviano, in Northern Italy, had fighter jets fly to the base of Mt. Bianco and the reports that Douglas read early the next morning made it sound like truly a portal to Hell had been opened. The fighters, alongside with Italian aircraft, were managing to barely keep the obscenities coming out of the portal at bay. Douglas had been in touch with the Russian military eventually, though it took time, as the routing was anything but straightforward, and they had to make sure both sides understood each other clearly. Douglas had not been idle and his measurements of the portal's scalar potentials and vortex rhythms gave him the idea that it should be able to shut down if it was hit with three much smaller tac nukes spaced two and a half seconds apart, and with HAARP modulating the resonating frequencies of the explosions very precisely. He also figured that in order to fool whatever intelligence had opened the portals, he would first instruct HAARP to keep a constant oscillating frequency on the portal. It had no practical effect, but it gave Douglas more information on how the scalar potentials adapted, which is what allowed him to work out the sequence. The Russians were the only ones that could do it with their hypersonic missiles, but the detonation yields had to be replaced with much lower ones as per his instructions, and that took time. He spent the time working out the same sort of solutions for the other portals around the world, wanting to avoid the large-scale destruction that the closing of the first portal on the Canadian-American border had resulted in.

Three days later, the first attempt at the Mt. Bianco portal failed. The second attempt later that day worked. There had been little need to evacuate anyone. The creatures that had escaped military action had already devastated the countryside's residents. The one bonus of this approach was that the "shockwave" with related appearance of all kind of creatures was limited to only 1,000 kilometres instead of the 3,000 miles of the American event, equivalent to nearly 5,000 kilometres, so he had reduced the effect to about a fifth of the diameter. Not great, but it was something. The Chinese portal was shut down later on the same day, with the loss of about half of Beijing from the detonations.

The position and weapons available to shut down the Chad portal were limited to the nuclear warheads available aboard a US aircraft carrier in the Mediterranean, and they did not have the ability to be as precise as the Russian weapons. Chad was hit by five, three hundred kiloton minutemen III, and it was only due to massive effects from HAARP on a wide band of frequencies that it worked. The teleportation diameter of the shock wave though had been enormous, like the American one, 3,000 miles.

The Australian portal and the one at the tip of South America would take longer to get within range of suitable missiles. Douglas could not do much beside pray and continually check the updates, although the numbers always came back the same. And there was another issue. The front of the "portal shockwave" was not too far from Monte Castello, so they should prepare for a surge of critters, and new kinds at that too.

In the last three years, Monte Castello had been heavily reinforced and returned somewhat to its original role as a medieval town, as had many old towns in Europe. Most people had opted to live within the walls unless they had the ability to heavily fortify their homes, as the Valenti and Douglas' families had. There were a few, but they all knew each other and they had all been warned that there would be an increase in activity after the slow decline that had taken place over the last three years.

No one ventured out alone, and usually only small groups of extremely well-armed men left the village, for necessary work, such as farming and collecting food.

No one knew what to expect, so most remained close to home. Taro Valenti was not one of them. His thinking was that one should try and see what was coming their way as early as possible instead of be surprised by it when it did.

He had fought with Jane about it because she wanted him to stay home. She had used every possible reasonable idea to get him to stay put, including spelling out that if he got eaten by a dragon, or whatever, she would be alone with five children and that was not something she wanted to face. He had explained that he knew what he was doing and he was only scouting, that's why he had the spotting scope with him, along with the Ruger Precision Rifle in .300 Win Mag. He had no intention of letting anything get close to him and he would go with two other men he had befriended in the meantime, Jordan Weir, a young man not yet 30, who had been on his honeymoon with his new wife Elizabeth, when the craziness had struck three years ago. They had remained in Monte Castello, in their AirBnB, since then, and had been helped by the locals. Being young, and the logistics on Earth having grossly disintegrated in large part, they had remained in Italy, and even had their first child two years ago. Because Taro spoke English fluently, and due to the large construction efforts at his home as well as Douglas', it was inevitable they would meet, and they did. Jordan offered to help with the construction or anything else that was needed. The young couple had little to no money left, and England was far and generally far less safe than mainland Europe had been. Despite werewolves, zombies, vampires, and other nasty creatures roaming the land there, the British government insisted that possession of firearms should remain strictly controlled. The traffic in weapons in the previously United Kingdom, which had now returned to being England, Wales, Scotland and Ireland, skyrocketed.

Along with food and silver, Jordan was "paid" by Taro with an older model shotgun that he had among the spares and a .45 Colt 1911, US government issue. One of four that Taro had retrieved from the bodies of US soldiers both at the time of the original appearance of the supernatural creatures, as well as after.

Jordan had proved himself to be brave, smart, and willing and able to learn anything Taro knew that he shared with him. He had become a trusted friend even though Taro was old enough to be his father. Jordan's wife Elizabeth and their little two-year-old Henry, were frequent guests at Taro's place, and sometime slept overnight at the house, which had been extended enough to allow for guests.

Over the last two years Jordan had also secured a little piece of land bordering Taro's and had it enclosed in Taro's general walling off of his land. They still lived at the AirBnB but had basically become permanent renters there, paying the owner in various products that were grown on Taro's farm. More recently, Jordan had finally acquired one of the more versatile weapons available, yet another SFAR Ruger assault rifle style weapon with decent glass on it and in the larger .308 calibre.

For the last six months, Jordan had often been along when Taro took nine-year old Marco shooting. Jordan had proved to be an excellent spotter and an accurate shooter.

The other man was also about the same age as Jordan and also English, he had ended up in Monte Castello, after he had heard that there was a link between the American base in Rimini and a presence of Sedevacantist Catholics even before the werewolves started appearing. Tony too had been a Sedevacantist before then, and had come through the last three years practically unscathed, which he had put down to his piety and devotion, since he offered a rosary every morning and every evening. He too had helped on Taro's farm and had purchased his own semi-automatic shotgun, a SPAS, which were difficult to come by, but he had acquired it when he bartered with an American in the Rimini base. Tony had taught the man how to serve at the Mass as one of the altar helpers, and the soldier had made one of the shotguns stored on the base go "missing". It was Tony's only weapon, aside his rosary with rather large crucifix, which he carried around his neck under his shirt. He also kept a small toy water pistol, but of very good quality, filled with holy water, in a small purpose-made holster on his belt.

They had left in the early morning, Taro had his converted ivory-handled .44 Magnum Dragoon, along with his Ruger Precision Rifle in .300 Winchester Magnum.

They had left the Humvee behind, and the three men had walked through fields and forests to get to the spot that Taro wanted to observe from, near the village of Monte Castello, but in a lightly forested ridge, it overlooked the hills and mountains further north.

There was still a hint of snow on the distant peaks, even though it was already well into spring. The mountains were a small part of the Apennines that made their way through most of central Italy.

As they sat down on the grass, Tony brought out a bottle of wine and some bread and salami from his backpack, and Jordan two large water bottles and some cheese. Taro's rifle was heavy and he always carried at least 100 rounds when he went out with it, and his left knee sometimes gave him trouble. Though the exercise of the last few years had in some way improved his fitness, after the age of fifty, things inevitably started to degrade a bit. As a result, Jordan carried most of the things they would need for the day-trip in his own backpack. Taro limited himself to his weapons, which also included a Gerber Mark II stiletto style knife, that had been blessed as well as had a small crucifix etched on its handle, and the ammunition in his small backpack. Jordan had the water, food and thermos of hot tea that Jane had made them while still angry and scared for her husband.

Taro walked all the way saying little, troubled by his wife's bad mood and lack of understanding. He knew she was afraid for him, and consequently for herself and their children should anything happen to him, but at the same time, he was disturbed by what he perceived as a lack of faith. After all, he had largely been responsible for having made Monte Castello one of the safest places to be, and thanks to Douglas, they had a very healthy relationship with the only people that could have really made the changes to their property that had taken place: The US military.

At root, his thought always came back to the same summarised conviction, tinged with a certain anger:

I am not going to die as a result of some fucking werewolf, disembodied spirit or even one of those terrifying Doppelgangers, for fuck's sake.

Besides, someone has to think ahead and be pro-active. Fights, wars, skirmishes, or whatever this was, were not won by the timid. And while he was not always a subscriber to the SAS's motto that "Who Dares Wins," especially given the more recent, less than stellar performances by these supposedly elite British soldiers, it was still a motto that in his experience certainly better reflected reality than to act as a scared rabbit whenever the choice presented itself.

With this somewhat subdued mood, which had spread as a kind of fog over the other two men, they settled down and Taro set up the spotting scope. While Jordan and Tony started to make sandwiches and taste the wine, Taro had started to observe the mountains, as he thought he had seen some movement there. It took him a moment to focus the strong portable scope, and when the image in it became clear, his mouth fell open a little, he had wanted to say something, but no words formed. What he was seeing was so far removed from anything he had imagined that he had no specific reaction. All the tribulations about Jane had immediately cleared from his head though.

At a distance of a few kilometres, on the edge of the snow-line on the nearest mountain, was a humanoid figure, the distance gave it a faintly blue tinge too, it was bare-chested and wearing some kind of loin-cloth and an extension of it, perhaps torn trousers, or maybe a kind of toga, and boots made of some material that could have been furs. The creature looked human to all intents and purposes, the problem was not how it looked, but its size. Even as Taro watched it, it picked up a rock the size of a small truck and hurled it at half-track that Taro now saw seemed to be firing a crew served machine gun at the giant. The distance made it hard to tell. He thought he saw a flicker of flame at the tip of the machine gun, just before the giant rock smashed directly into the half-track, crushing it and flinging it off the road with a somersault. The whole scene had been soundless. The wind was blowing towards the giant, so probably the sounds had difficulty travelling this far. Taro continued to watch through the spotting scope and tried to estimate the size of the bearded giant, comparing it to the half-track that had been swept off the road and behind some terrain now, so he worked from memory and thought that the giant must be at least eight or nine metres in height, and probably over ten. He tried to see if there were any other landmarks near it that he could use as a reference, but in doing so, all he saw was two more giants appear, walking towards the first one. One had a double-headed axe in its hands, that was probably as long as a car, and in the same kind of style of clothing, only with a giant fur or blanket, covering the torso, indeed as a sort of toga. The other had a more traditional set of trousers and boots, which also seemed reminiscent of what one might assume ancient Vikings might have worn. This one had also more covering on the upper half of the body, and carried a shield in one hand and a gigantic sword in the other.

Taro watched them in silence for a bit, then he moved away from the scope and signalled to Jordan to look through it.

As Jordan peered through the scope, he whispered a *fuck*, in unmasked awe.

"Tony, take a look," he said, making room for the other man to switch places with him.

Tony took a few seconds to adjust, and when he saw them simply said:

"Giants. Three of them," then he turned to look at Taro and Jordan and returned to pouring some wine in the three cups he had packed in his bag.

Jordan and Taro glanced at each other.

"Autists for the coolness award, I guess," said Jordan, teasingly.

Tony looked up, an unspoken question on his face, he responded.

"What? It's three giants."

"Yes, but most people would be a little awed at least," said Taro.

"*You* didn't say anything," responded Tony with the precision of the neuro-atypical.

"I didn't want to spoil the surprise, Tony."

"Well, yes, it's quite strange, certainly." Said Tony calmly, as he took a bite of the salami sandwich he had made.

"But then again, these are strange times," he continued after swallowing, and then he took another bite. Calmly.

Taro looked at Jordan. "Autists. Unflappable or neurotic. Accept no substitutes."

Jordan snickered.

"Well, there is no point in panicking, or freaking out, they are far, they will take a while to get here, and in the meanwhile, we can observe them and prepare, which is why we came out here in the first place." It was all very correct, logical and true, of course.

"Do you only see in grayscale too?" asked Taro.

"Colours are heresy after the gays appropriated the rainbow, don't you know," teased Jordan looking at Taro.

"Oh, fuck off, both of you," said Tony, then continued, "go prancing about as colourfully as you like while you expound at length on the shock, awe, and majesty of murderous giants, if it makes you all feel better."

"It's not that, Tony, it's just that we are sad for your apparent lack of ability to be able to enjoy the strangeness of these times," said Jordan.

"Well, these times are mostly terrible, with rampant evil in the forms of vicious monsters spread throughout the land. I am thoroughly enjoying this fine wine though, sitting here on the side of a mountain, with my two good friends, on a clear spring day, observing giants through a telescope at a safe distance." He sipped from his plastic cup.

"Fair enough," said Jordan, giving up his attempt at trying to grasp Tony's apparent lack of emotion. It's not as if either he or Taro had displayed much of it either, but there was a different sense to it; Taro was controlled, and his ability to take things in stride did not translate in any lack of emotion. Jordan was similar. With Tony, however, he suspected seeing giants, or having a nice clear day, was probably on the same plane, as far as appreciation or surprise went. Tony's somewhat different perspective made him very reliable in many respects, but at times his perception of things baffled Jordan and amused Taro.

"Do you think our rifles would work against them?" asked Jordan of Taro, but without looking at him; he was staring towards the mountains, as he finished assembling his own sandwich. Even with the naked eye, you could still see a little movement, even if not distinct enough to really tell what it was.

Taro thought for a few second before answering. Tony too waited for the older man to speak. Taro had far more experience of shooting at things than either of them, or even of both combined.

"Well, a .300 Win Mag in the head is probably enough to kill one, I should think. After all, it is enough to kill an elephant, if you hit it just right, but my dad always used a .460 Weatherby for elephants, and even buffalo." He paused, thinking about it a bit more.

"Would a shotgun even do anything to it?" asked Tony.

"Or my .308?" said Jordan, patting his rifle, which lay across his legs.

"A shotgun… maybe. If you had a solid slug in it and fired it from only a few metres away into its eyeball. Maybe even the forehead. The problem is that in order to be that close, one of those guys can probably pick up a handful of rocks and fling it at you, and it would have the same effect on a person as being hit by what your people, a few hundred years ago, called "grapeshot" out of the mouths of cannons."

Jordan and Tony nodded silently, as Taro spoke up again.

"Buckshot… I personally would avoid shooting it at one of those things, if I had any option at all, because unless you get really lucky, I think it would just piss one off."

"That's what I figured," replied Tony.

"As for the .308, again, I think a headshot would work, but I probably would not want to be more than a hundred metres away or so," said Taro.

"And with your rifle?" asked Tony, always preferring precise numbers when he could get them.

Taro thought about it a little.

"I don't know, I'd have to check the force, not sure off the top of my head, but I would not want to be firing at one of those things further out than five hundred metres or so."

"That's a pretty safe distance," said Jordan, "and your rifle is set for that, right?"

"Yes, zeroed it at five hundred meters."

"How hard would it be to hit one in the head at that distance?" asked Tony.

"Not hard for me. I have practiced a lot. If he stood still for a second or two, I'd say always, unless I get a flier. But I make sure to load the .300 Win Mag rounds with absolute precision, so it's unlikely. If he was walking, I'd say I'd hit him maybe nine out of ten times. Eight, worst case scenario." He paused a bit, then added, "Running and dodging…" he made a face, and before he could continue Jordan added:

"Prrrrrrrr…." The sound of a fart of fear escaping a rectum.

"Running and dodging and throwing handfuls of rocks at you," said Tony.

"Then I'd want a minigun," replied Taro, "which I am sorry to say, we don't have."

They all sat in silence for a bit, then, as each man thought of the giants in turn, they came to the same conclusions if in different ways. It was Tony that voiced it first.

"So, what do we do? We can't wait for them to come here."

"No, we cannot." Taro's words had a finality to them.

"They can probably throw big boulders too," said Jordan.

"Yes, they can. I didn't tell you guys but when I first saw the giant, he had a huge rock, the size of a car, maybe, he flung it at a half-track and smashed it off the track or kind of road you see there. It bounced behind terrain, so you can't see it anymore." Taro was thinking of the poor bastards that had been in that half-track. He wondered if any survived.

"You saw that?" asked Tony.

"Yes," replied Taro sombrely. There was silence for a little while.

"*Fuck,*" whispered Jordan again.

At the Valenti house, Jane was talking with Elizabeth who had brought their two-year old to play with Jane and Taro's children. Although older, all the girls loved what they referred to as "the baby." Marco, the only boy, played along, but was not as taken with little children he wasn't directly related to, though he liked little Henry.

"I just worry, and Taro, is such a mule-headed man, he acts as if I am just irritating him for no reason!" Jane was venting to Elizabeth, who was almost half Jane's age. A beautiful and intelligent young woman, she was deeply in love with her own husband, Jordan, and trusted him implicitly. Jane was aware of it, but in the back of her mind also thought of it as "the innocence of youth".

"I know, you worry, but Jordan is with him, and those two guys together can probably survive almost anything. Plus, they have Tony too." As they spoke, Elizabeth was helping Jane make lasagne.

"They are not invincible." It had come out of her mouth before she could stop it. She looked at Elizabeth and apologised.

"I'm sorry, you're right. I don't want my paranoia to spread to you. You probably have the right attitude for this new world of monsters."

"It's not that I don't worry. I just have faith that Jordan will overcome whatever comes his way."

"And if it's a horde of monsters?" Jane could not help it, that first encounter with the werewolf that Taro had survived only by some miracle still gave her nightmares, three years later.

Elizabeth, perspicacious, watching Jane, thought to ask her something pertinent.

"Do you not believe in God?"

Jane glanced at her like a deer in headlights for a brief second before replying.

"Perhaps not as much as you."

"It's not a question of degree though. Either you do or you do not." Elizabeth paused, to let Jane digest it.

"And if you do, then you do it with your whole heart. And then you may have a worry, a shadow of fear, but it is only that, a little shadow, because inside you have a true knowledge of God. And since God loves us, all is going to work out, no matter what happens."

Jane looked at the young woman before her, a redhead with beautiful features, she had recovered almost immediately from her pregnancy, and being Sedevacantist Catholics she assumed there would soon be another child along.

Sedevacantism, or actual Catholicism, being the only religion that seemed to have things and rituals that had real effects against some of the undead type of creatures that had come through the portals, had spread around the Earth like a wild fire. No one even referred to the Novus Ordo impostors as "Catholics" any further. A real Pope had not yet been pronounced or elected, due to the difficulties, but everyone knew that when the word *Catholic* was used now, it meant the actual Catholics, not the ones that had pretended to be such since 1958, and until things from a Hellish realm, proved beyond doubt that only the real sacraments of the Church, not the "modernised" fake ones, had effect against the various vampires and other supernatural things.

"I was not raised Catholic, or even Christian of any kind. I know your parents too were not Catholics, but they taught you about God and Christianity and raised you a Christian. It was different for me, and at a time and in a place where the lies and degeneracy of the world was considered normal. It's still difficult sometimes to believe all of this," she moved the wooden spoon she was stirring the sauce with in a slow arc, "is really going on."

Elizabeth only smiled at Jane.

"And yet, you're right. It's undeniable."

Then Jane said: "I am a terrible Christian," dejectedly.

"No, you are not. I can't imagine what it must have been like for you. It must have been very difficult."

"Well, that's no excuse. Taro too had no Christian upbringing at all, but he figured it out and he became a Catholic long before all this madness. I was baptised with him and we married in a Church, but mostly I think I followed and believed him, more than the Church."

"Well," said Elizabeth, looking at Jane meaningfully, "So? Keep doing it. It's how I became a Catholic, following my husband. And your husband helped too, all that talking they did while working on the farm. Sometimes I think the monsters only played a very small part in convincing Jordan."

"That's what I mean," said Jane, a sense of some guilt assailing her a little as she spoke, "Taro figured it out and believed fully before any of this stuff. And because of it he figured out how to kill the werewolves and other things before anyone else. But I don't know how he does it. He is so…"

"Mule-headed?" asked Elizabeth smiling.

Jane laughed, "Yes."

"Still, even mules can be right about stuff."

"Clearly." She stirred the sauce some more, then said, "Still, I just don't seem to be able to get that same sense of certainty. And I always wonder, but *what if*… Taro says it's a kind of sin, or a mind-worm, a hint of rebelliousness towards… God, him, the universe as a whole, or something like that. He's probably right."

"Oh no. No, I don't think so at all," said Elizabeth.

Jane just assumed Elizabeth was being polite, and mentally dismissed the words, but Elizabeth noticed, and carried on speaking.

"It's normal for us women to think that way."

Jane looked at her with a raised eyebrow questioningly, "But you just said a minute ago… you are certain, you don't have doubt…"

"Yes," replied the younger woman, because I trust God and my husband, both. I mean Jordan is still human, he will make mistakes, but so do we all, that's not important."

"But what if one of those mistakes kills them?" asked Jane a little exasperated.

"Well, then they will be with God, and somehow things will still work out. Not great, and I hope it never happens, but ultimately if you are with God, well… you are with God."

"And that is where my doubt comes in," replied Jane, tired and a little sad at her own indecision at times.

"No, it doesn't. You believe deep down, inside." Elizabeth's words cut through the fog. Jane heard them clear and certain.

"How do you know?"

"Because you do. We all do. Those who let fear take hold may doubt, but we all *know*. We are born knowing."

"Maybe not me. Maybe not everyone."

"Really? I don't think so. I think if you stop and ask yourself, you know God is real and true and loves us."

"Maybe…"

"Not maybe. Your first answer is really yes, right? Then your mind intrudes and makes you ask ten million questions. The *what ifs* you mentioned. Right?"

"Yes," said Jane, looking at this young woman that seemed to be wise well beyond her years.

"But how do you not have those thoughts?"

"Oh, no, it's impossible not to have them. We all have them."

Jane paused and looked at the girl for a bit. She'd stopped stirring the sauce too.

"You have them?"

"Oh sure, but not often, I learnt long ago to let go of them, like shadows."

"How do you do that?"

"It's a choice, you just ignore it. Like you know, do you ever have a bad thought, like. 'oh, what if my child falls while learning to walk and really hurts itself or dies', stuff like that?"

"Sure…"

"And do you pay such thoughts any mind?"

"Not usually, no, because usually they are absurd, but other thoughts…"

"It's the same. Fearful thoughts are all the same. Fear is not real, it's an illusion, always."

"Taro says that!"

"I know, he told Jordan, and Jordan told me. It's true."

"Or maybe my husband is just a really good cult leader and he's brainwashed all of you!" Said Jane sarcastically.

"Cool. Just think how powerful that would be!" Replied Elizabeth smiling.

Jane looked at her in mock horror, "Oh my God, it's true, he's brainwashed you all!"

"But the holy water and silver bullets work," replied Elizabeth with not a little glee in her eyes.

Jane shook her head.

"Yeah, you're right. I'm just a bad Christian; and a bad wife."

"No, you're not. You're just helping Taro be better."

Jane was honestly surprised.

"How so?"

"Well, by having to deal with your doubts he inevitably must refine his appreciation of Christianity, which in turn makes it easier for him to explain it to others."

"Ohhhh, that's good. And it will also drive him mad. Think you can tell him that when he gets back?"

They laughed and changed topic. But a little later, when they expected the men back and the children were starting to look hungry as they helped set the table, Jane brought it up again.

"I still wish I had your certainty."

"You do. You married Taro."

Jane was a little confused by that simple statement.

"What do you mean?"

"Well, look at him… he's misanthropic, often speaks in ways that would make a drunken sailor blush, he is perceived by almost everyone to be a man with no patience or tolerance for slow wit, errors, or wasted time, and even if over half a century old, he tends to keep going longer and harder than most men twenty years younger." She paused to let Jane digest it for a half-second, then finished with:

"Only a supreme act of faith bordering on full-blown insanity would let any woman marry a guy like that!"

"I know, right?! It's what I keep telling him too!" Said Jane cheerfully.

Elizabeth went calm and suddenly had a very serious face, before she spoke again.

"No, Jane. Really. I'm serious."

Jane stood silently and serious for a little bit too. Then she burst out laughing. As did Elizabeth.

By the time the men returned, Jane's mood had changed and she was ready to help dispel the haze of fearfulness that had hung over her since the discussion with Taro in the morning. Taro noticed and while they all sat at the large table for lunch, he was especially attentive, saying please and thank you, and meaning it, instead of just saying the words, and touching her when she passed close by, grabbing her and giving her a quick little kiss. She returned it and was similarly sweet, but she could feel Taro still had some tension in him, and she wanted to dispel it, but she would wait until they were alone.

Douglas and Kate had also been called over and along with their three children, they joined in for lunch and the news of the giants too. While the small mob of children ate and played in the large playroom, the adults sat and ate at the main table, occasionally interrupted by the squeals and games of the five Valenti children, the three Jones' ones, and the one Weir child.

They had a nice meal, and laughed, drank, and ate well, before finishing with an espresso. Then Taro brought up the inevitable.

He had already explained about the giants they had seen and what they could do. The women looked worried, as did Anna, Scarlet, and Marco, who along with John, Douglas' boy, the same age as Marco, and Mary-Lou, his seven-year old daughter, had listened fascinated as soon as they had heard the word "giants". Arianna and Alina, along with Douglas' four-year old Robert did not seem worried at all.

"Anyway, the point is, we can't wait for them to come here," said Taro with a certain finality.

"Is that why you're nervous still?" asked Jane.

Taro looked at his wife. Her blue eyes intelligent and penetrating as the first time he'd seen them.

"You know what it means?" asked Taro, with a tired look in his own eyes.

Jane's eyes took on that quality they sometimes did, as if they had become somehow brighter in a way that could be sensed if not seen.

"You're going to go out and attack them first."

Taro only kept looking at her in silence, but the tiredness of spirit had left him suddenly. She knew. She understood. It filled him with the energy that men gain when the woman they chose to be with saw into them and believed in them without doubt.

He nodded slowly; never taking his eyes off hers.

"I'm sorry about this morning. I know you're right." She said it without wavering or hiding anything.

Taro nodded again, acknowledging her apology. And her. Her understanding, and trust.

"Want to know about it?"

Jane hesitated before replying, "Whatever you think is best."

Taro nodded again, then explained his plan concisely and directly. The questions from the children were endless nevertheless, and Douglas excused himself to make a radio call to the base in Rimini. They had to be prepared too.

When Douglas returned to the table, he did not have the best news.

"They would only give me one. And that because I said I needed it myself."

"Well, you do!" Said Taro, irritated.

"Yeah, but I figure you need it more. Because you're not going to let me come with you, are you?"

Taro shrugged and opened his hands. It was a silent version of saying: *you know why.*

Douglas nodded. *Yes, I know why. I am indispensable, because of my understanding of the scalar physics. Dammit.*

The requested equipment was with them within the hour. And Taro spent the next hour calibrating it, while Jordan familiarised himself with Taro's Ruger Precision Rifle, and Tony with Jordan's Ruger Assault Rifle.

By the time they finished it was heading towards four in the afternoon.

They still had enough daylight to get back to the ridge and see if they could find where the giants might be now.

Before they set off, Taro had taken Jane up to their bedroom, ostensibly to get his heavier jacket, as towards nightfall the temperature still dropped, but in reality, just to give her a proper kiss. A way to let her know he would stay alive and be back. Before heading back down to the others he told her, "Don't worry."

She smiled and replied "I won't."

He was sure she was not necessarily telling him the whole truth, but he'd learnt to accept her sometimes infuriating and sometimes endearing Englishness as best he could. This aspect, the putting on a brave face, and really meaning it too, not just pretending, was one of the qualities he loved most about her.

He gave her another quick kiss, before saying "I'll see you later tonight."

"Okay."

Trepidation, faith, love, and ultimately a belief in me too, is in that little word, he thought. He smiled, then turned and left.

5

They had taken the Humvee this time, and back on the ridge they set up and started to scan the horizon both with the spotting scope as well as a pair of more traditional binoculars or the scopes on their weapons.

The terrain was hilly and forested though, and they could not see any of the giants initially. It was Tony that had spotted what he thought might be some movement of tree-tops that looked a bit too rough to be caused by a breeze.

"Over there," he pointed ahead. Both Taro and Jordan put their face to the scopes on their weapons. But neither saw what Tony was referring to. There was the edge of a forest some half a kilometre away and Taro was focusing on that when the image in his scope was suddenly blocked. He opened his left eye in reflex and then he saw it.

He had assumed Tony was talking about something a lot further away. He had not been. A giant that looked for all the world like a magnified version of a bearded Viking with an axe was now only about two hundred metres in front of them, and as Taro registered this, another giant head appeared next to it, on the giant's right side. They were obviously climbing a hill and coming towards them. If the giants started running they would be on top of the three men in seconds. The giants had a slightly blue-tinge to their skin. Taro felt the grip of fear enter him, but he pushed it aside as he had learnt to do in years of training in martial arts and working dangerous jobs in Africa.

"Jordan, aim at the head of the one with the axe, wait to fire until I do. Remember to compensate for the distance they are only about two hundred meters away. Aim at the bottom of his chin."

The .300 was zeroed at five hundred metres, as was Taro's temporary new weapon, but he knew his own rifle like a part of him, this thing he now aimed at the giant behind the one with the axe he had only sighted in a short while ago and he was not as familiar with the ballistics of the rounds it fired. He had to make a quick decision, and he did not bother to calculate things, he guesstimated it and aimed at the mouth of the giant. Both were still walking. Taro didn't hesitate or think too much, he fired instinctively, and the report of the .50 calibre Barrett sniper weapon he had got through Douglas' connection with the base in Rimini was loud enough to make Jordan's ears as well as Tony's ring. None of them had been wearing ear protection.

Jordan fired a half second after, trying to ignore the ringing in his head even as it hit him. Tony, standing, unlike Taro and Jordan who had been prone and using the bipods on their respective rifles, started firing too, quickly and repeatedly.

The giant with the shield and sword was the one Taro had fired at. The .50 calibre bullet hit him square in the connection between nose and skull, shattering it and going straight through the giant's skull, taking a good chunk of it out the back of its head. Taro saw the impact by way of noting a dark spray behind the head of the giant. He reloaded the bolt action weapon as fast as he could.

Jordan's shot had been equally well placed and entered the axe wielder's right eye, but the giant had begun to turn its head, to look at the one Taro had shot, so Jordan's shot took out its eye and came out the side of its head, but did not kill the creature.

Tony had been firing at the third giant that neither Taro not Jordan had seen, being as they were looking through their scopes and had a reduced field of vision. To the right of the giant Jordan had wounded, a bit further away, was the one that had thrown the rock at the half-track. It did not have a weapon in its hands, but it started running at the small group, and Tony had started firing the SFAR at it. Rapid semi-automatic fire meant he had shot five rounds at it before Taro or Jordan had reloaded and started to adjust. Jordan had not changed target, and fired at the axe wielder again, but this time he aimed for the chest, as he wanted to make sure he at least hit the thing and he was not sure he would hit the head now that the creature was twisting about as it made a roaring scream of pain while holding the right side of its head, where its eye used to be, with its left hand across its face.

Taro had heard the reports from Tony and while reloading noted the other giant running at them. He had maybe three seconds left to shoot, he scooted the whole heavy rifle to the right, while also pushing off the ground and getting into a weird, half-sitting position, with his left leg bent under him and the right one splayed out. He lifted the Barrett and shouldered it but did not put his eye to the scope, he held his head high and just sighted the weapon by pointing it at the giant rushing them, aiming for centre mass, and he fired. The muzzle break of the .50 was now even more towards Jordan who had been prone beside Taro, and the report physically hurt Jordan who —in a macabre reflection of the giant he had fired twice on— now snatched his left hand up to his own left ear, as his eardrum and Vagus nerve sent signals of distress to his brain.

Tony kept firing, and as Taro dropped the stock to his thigh as he worked the .50's bolt he saw the impacts on the giant's chest as dust puffs. The creature had stopped and looked at its chest when Taro had fired, then the smaller impact of Tony's rifle seemed to register. The creature was huge, now only about fifty metres away, it was physically frightening to see it this close. It was taller than the small copse of olive trees it was in now, some ten meters or so high, it's blue-tinted bare chest enormous and the puffs of dust appearing on it not seeming to have much effect, but as Taro rammed another round in the chamber and lifted the weapon again, he also saw a darker spot on the left breast, this may have been where his first round had hit.

Shit. He thought. *A lung shot.* Taro knew a man could run a long distance with a lung shot. And this thing had strides that meant it would be on them in a few steps.

As he shouldered the rifle again, the giant looked up from its chest and directly at Taro. Their eyes met, because Taro was thinking of going for a head shot, even if not being able to use the scope due to the size of the giant and the short distance. The malice in the thing's eyes was a mixture of hatred, rage and what Taro could only think of as raw evil. Something that hated humanity as a whole, or perhaps Taro specifically. It was frightening because of the size of the monster and the implication of sudden and inescapable death that its proximity implied. There were no conscious thoughts left in Taro's mind then; only instinct.

He had entered what the ancient samurai Miyamoto Musashi had labelled *The Void* in his Book of Five Rings. A state of being where there was no fear, no desire, only a perfection of action. Taro had entered this state only a very few times in his life, each one of them had been a life-threatening situation. He squeezed the trigger and he did not perceive the report of the weapon, as if sound was no longer a part of his reality. He saw the dark spot appear on the right cheek of the giant, on the edge of its huge hay-coloured beard, and the thing's head turned to the right a bit. Everything happened as if time had slowed down for Taro. He felt a sense of accomplishment, not pride or joy exactly, more like a simple noticing of efficiency. He started to reload the gun again, the giant took another step towards them, then slowly started to buckle, and fell forward, its body partially crushing an olive tree on its way down. It didn't put a hand out. It fell with its face plainly hitting the grassy Earth with a thud that was felt as a vibration through the Earth.

And suddenly time was back at normal speed. As Taro ejected the round, an object that was huge flew right between him and Jordan and close enough to Tony to throw him off balance and have Tony's last round fire dangerously above Jordan's head as he fell to the ground. Some Earth and a tufts of grass were still floating in the air a few metres in front of Taro and Jordan, where the object must have briefly touched the ground. Taro looked at the giant Jordan had shot in the eye and saw it no longer had the axe. Jordan had reloaded despite the pain and whistling in his ear and fired again. Taro saw the giant's head snap back but it stood

46

still, not falling. Jordan reloaded again, Taro finished closing his own bolt too but waited to see what Jordan's next round would do. Tony was trying to get back on his feet and being sure to point his rifle away from Jordan. Checking his rifle, Tony saw he was out of ammunition, so he started to eject the ten round magazine he had emptied by firing at the giant that had now fallen too close to them for his comfort.

Jordan fired again, aiming through the scope, he had taken his time, a couple of seconds. The giant's head snapped back again but this time did not return to its position and instead the monster continued falling backward, until it landed, like the first one Taro had killed, below the rise that had originally hidden them from view until they had started walking up it.

It was over.

"Everyone okay?" asked Taro.

Tony was reloading and didn't reply. Jordan reloaded the .300 and looking around said, "Yes, except I think when you fired that cannon next to my ear some of my brain leaked out the other side."

"Sorry about that. Sucks, I know. My dad did a similar thing to me when we hunted buffalo in Africa once. Still, beats being stomped by a giant."

"Barely," said Jordan holding his ear. Then, looking around he saw the other giant lying on the grass. Its head just some thirty-five metres from them. He froze for a few seconds before speaking.

"What… where did he come from?" Jordan had been so focused on the giant he had killed that he had not even been aware there was another one of them running up to them.

"There were three of them," said Taro calmly. "It's why I had to scramble to shoot at it as it ran at us and you had the muzzle break of this thing blowing hot gasses at your ear almost directly."

"I didn't even..." said Jordan, before trailing off. He was disturbed he had not even been aware of the third giant.

"It happens," said Taro. "Adrenaline, lots going on, you get tunnel vision. Brain tends to focus only on the immediate threat."

"You saw it?" asked Jordan looking around to Taro.

"Tony did. He started firing at it right away and as I looked up saw it was running at us. They are so big and fast... it was nearly too late. Thank God Douglas got us this .50. Without it I think we would be bug paste by now."

Tony had finished reloading now and spoke up.

"I emptied my magazine at it. I don't think it even slowed it down."

"I think it did. Maybe would even have killed it... in time, but not fast enough. Even my first shot I think only punched through its lung, assuming they have lungs, and didn't stop it right away."

Jordan suddenly shifted his weight and turned around, looking behind Taro and Tony, and in a somewhat alarmed tone said, "Hey! Who are you? Show yourself!"

Taro spun round but left the Barrett on his lap and reached for his Colt Dragoon instead. But he saw nothing except more olive trees.

Jordan had stood up and held his rifle in both hands but not pointing it, just across his legs and shouted in badly accented Italian "Chi va là? Parla!" *Who goes there? Talk!*

But there was no reply.

Taro looked at Jordan and jerked his head by way of asking a question.

"I don't know, there was a guy standing there, watching us."

"Where exactly," said Taro.

"Behind those trees, he went off to the left."

Tony had drawn his water pistol loaded with holy water and Taro shouldered the heavy Barrett and drew his Colt Dragoon. Jordan held on to the rifle. Together they headed at a brisk pace towards where Jordan had seen the man standing. As they walked in that direction Taro noticed what seemed like a trail or some kind of periodic gouging of the Earth going off towards where they had left the Humvee closer to the little country road that had taken them close to the ridge. He pointed it out to Jordan and Tony, but Jordan indicated the person he had seen had gone off to the left. Taro nodded and pointing at Jordan and Tony indicated they should continue in that direction. Then he pointed to himself and indicated the trail, but did a looping motion with his hand. He would follow that trail a bit then make a loop and catch up with them shortly.

Jordan had his Colt 1911 too, but Taro didn't want to leave them alone long, he just wanted to see what the trail was and if it had any connection to whatever Jordan had seen. It did not take him long to see the cause and the final effect of that strange trail. He called out loudly to both men by name when he saw it.

They came up shortly, they had clearly jogged and were looking worried, but Taro was calm. Leaning against the Humvee, the .50 cal with its butt on the ground and the barrel resting against it too, next to him.

The giant's axe was embedded midway into the Humvee. The vehicle was almost sheared in half, with one side of the double headed axe fully inside the cabin space. The shaft of the weapon aimed into the sky at a high angle.

"Fuck." Said Jordan calmly.

"Is that what knocked me to the ground?" asked Tony.

"I think you came within a giant's ass hair's width of becoming a slice of breakfast food for them, Tony," replied Taro.

"Fuck," repeated Jordan, "that's an amazing throw. It must be almost a thousand feet!"

"Closer to seven-hundred fifty I think," said Taro. "About two hundred and fifty metres or so. Maybe a little more."

"Let's count it in steps," said Tony.

Taro and Jordan nodded to Tony's idea. As they started to walk off Taro said, "I see you fuckers are all torn up about my Humvee too."

"Yeah, that sucks, Taro," replied Jordan, "but honestly, I am just so glad I haven't shat myself through all this, that losing the Humvee doesn't seem so bad."

Taro nodded in agreement. Still, he didn't think he'd get another one from the Americans. *Then again,* he thought, *I don't plan on returning the Barrett either, so it might even out.*

They made their way to the giant bodies down the hill first.

The knock at the door was unexpected.

Jane went to see who was there through the outside camera, while Alina, always eager to greet her father, had climbed one of the cupboards near the barred window, to see who was at the outside door. It was Taro, but he didn't have his pack, rifle, or revolver on his hip. Jane hesitated a second or two. Had something happened?

"Not daddy."

Jane turned to see Alina pointing outside, while she looked through the window, and the hair on the back of her neck stood on end.

"Get away from the window baby!" She rushed to pick Alina up bodily and putting her back down on the floor.

"That's not daddy, mommy," said the little girl, looking at her mother's blue eyes with her own, equally blue.

"I know. I think I know, darling. Go get Anna and tell her to bring the radio," replied Jane, as she grabbed the pump-action Winchester from the rack near the main door and checked it was loaded with silver buckshot that also had holy water bubbles in each buckshot.

Anna entered the room with a large walkie-talkie and a questioning look on her face.

"Hey babe, open the door, it's me. There was some trouble. I lost the equipment and the guys."

Taro's voice came through the closed double door set-up they had on each entrance to the home loud and clear.

"Dad?" Said Anna concerned.

"Radio your father. Channel four." Said Jane as she shouldered the shotgun but kept it pointing at the ground a few feet from the front door."

"But… he's outside…"

"No, I don't think so. Radio him," said Jane, tense.

"But…"

"Not daddy!" Said Alina, looking at Anna with a very serious and scalding look on her little face. Anna had a soft spot for all her sisters, but Alina being the smallest at only five years of age was the one that made her laugh the most with her ways.

"Oh… okay Alina, I'll call him." She switched on the radio as the voice of Taro came through the door again.

"Babe, come on, it's bad, they are not far behind me and I have no weapons on me, open the door, quickly!"

Jane felt as if she may faint from a mixture of fear, tension and a sense she might be losing her mind.

"Dad? Come in, over." Anna had called but looked anxiously at the door and Jane in a posture of looking ready to shoot if the door opened. The front door was solid steel and immediately on the outside of it had been build an area that was essentially similar to a shark cage, made of heavy metal bars that encompassed the entire front door and some space around it. Making it an area from which the outside world could be observed, while preventing it from entering through the front door. The cage too had a very strong door, though this one was not solid, as it was made of welded bars with gaps between them.

"Jane, please, can you just open the door, I am defenceless here!"

"Yes? What's wrong, Over?"

Taro's voice had come through both from immediately outside the house as well as the walkie-talkie.

Jane motioned for Anna to come closer to her.

"Hold the button in," she said to Anna, then when the girl did, she spoke.

"Taro, where are you? Over."

"I'm… up on the ridge. What is the problem?" *He'd forgotten to say over,* thought Jane. Looking at Anna she nodded for the button to be pressed again.

"Taro, I need to know if you and Jordan and Tony are okay. Can you put them on?"

Taro, on the other end, busy examining dead giants was irritated. *Probably Elizabeth worrying about Jordan, or Jane worrying, or some damned thing. What the hell was the point of them interrupting us here, damn it!*

"Tony, just take the radio and tell them we are all okay. Let Jordan speak too." He bit his tongue, preventing himself from saying *fucking women*, in frustration. Tony would not have approved. And he was right. *I need to try and swear a smidgen less. And be kinder. They are probably just worried.* He started to feel bad about his short temper. He'd be nice when he got back home.

"Hi Jane, Tony here. And Jordan. Jordan say hello." There was a pause on the radio then, a laconic "Hello?" then another pause, "Over."

"So, Taro and you Tony, and Jordan are all okay, and on the ridge, looking out for giants? Over."

Taro gesticulated quickly to Tony indicating no, no, silence, or something... Tony couldn't tell, so he handed the walkie-talkie back to Taro, who he could tell was getting irritated at being interrupted from their investigation of the dead giants.

"Hey babe, it's me. Yes, we are all okay, what's going on? Why are you calling? Over." He had spoken fast.

Jane on the other end recognised her husband's impatience in his voice. He was trying to be nice about it, but he probably figured her radioing was scaring away his chance to bag a giant or something. *Fucking men,* she thought.

"I'm calling because there is another you standing outside telling me to let him in. Over." *See if you're irritated now, hubby!*

"Don't open that fucking door! That's not me! It's one of those fucking body doubles that eat children! Over?!"

Jane could hear the panic in Taro's voice and she suddenly felt bad for having got irritated at his impatience. He was far away and his family was in danger. It must be a horrible feeling. She hadn't meant to cause it.

"Okay babe, I am not opening the door to the thing outside." As she finished saying it, she could hear the other Taro banging on the bars outside.

"Jane, let me in! They are coming!"

But how does it know my name?! The thought was sudden and terrifying. She thought fast, then took the radio from Anna and made sure it was not sending, and she shouted through the door,

"Okay babe, just tell me how many carats was the engagement ring you gave me?"

The Taro outside the door spoke up with a little more urgency and fear in his voice.

"What? What the fuck babe, open the door, I can see them in the forest, they are coming!"

"Taro," she felt bad using his name, but it had to be done, "I am not opening the door until you tell me how many carats my engagement ring was."

"What the hell babe, I am going to die here!"

She pushed the send button to talk on the radio and spoke again:

"Taro, how many carats was the engagement ring you gave me? Over."

The reply came instantly.

"Point eight-eight of a carat. Two inclusions, a light one near the middle, that's you, and a dark one near the edge, that's me. And I don't remember the official clarity but it's the best one you can get, apart from the two inclusions. Over."

"Thanks babe," replied Jane on the radio, then she opened the front door, shouldered the shotgun and shot the Taro outside the cage door in the face.

Anna screamed in terror and covered her face, looking at Jane as if the woman had morphed into a monster herself.

Alina walked calmly up to her mother, then a little past her, and looked at the now faceless dead body whose head was mostly a pool of brain matter and red ooze and whose clothing and boots and entire body was now shifting, as if melting into a humanoid form that resembled more the texture of a giant amoeba with octopus-like texture and ridges along its four main appendages.

"Not daddy." She said calmly. Then came back inside and shut the door.

Anna was still freaked out and looking at Alina and Jane as if they were both monsters.

"It wasn't your father Anna. Go look. It's some kind of shape-shifting thing."

Anna held her chest and sat down at the table instead. She could hardly speak.

"Oh my God. I nearly died. I think my heart nearly exploded. I thought you'd shot dad."

"No darling, I only fantasise about it sometimes, I would never really do it."

Anna looked up at Jane still in shock. "Not funny mom!" She was still shaking.

"What is going on there? I'm coming, but the Humvee is destroyed, I have to run, it will take a while. Over."

Jane picked up the radio from the table again and replied.

"It's ok babe. I just shot you in the face with a shotgun. And you changed into your true form. A kind of giant slimy snail. Over."

"What? What the fuck?! Did you open the fucking door? Over!"

"Only the inner door babe. In order to shoot it... you... you know... Over."

"Jane, what the fuck! I told you to not open the door. Now how do I know it's you and not a fucking family of shapeshifters when I get back? Over!"

"Ask me a question. Or many questions, of things only you and I know. That's what I did. Over."

There was a couple of seconds of pause.

"The diamond? Over."

"Yeah. It didn't know shit about that. But it knew my name. How did it know my name babe? Over."

"I have no fucking idea. Wait. You only asked it one question? Over."

"One's all I need babe. Over."

"What the fuck? What if I had forgotten some detail of the diamond? You would have just blown me away! Over!"

"Oh darling... if you forgot the care and detail you put into designing my engagement ring it would mean you had stopped loving me, and what good to me would you be then anyway, eh? Over." Jane was smiling at the radio, but in truth her knees felt weak and her own heart rate was still high.

Anna, watching, thought: *Better not piss mom off too much! The woman might not just have a very dark sense of humour. She might be insane!* Her heartbeat was still over 100 beats a minute too.

After a few further communications back and forth over the radio made it clear the Valenti home was still secure, Taro, Jordan and Tony decided to finish examining the dead giants, before heading back on foot. The giant with the sword and shield had a pouch tied to its belt. It was the size of a large sack and took them a while to untie from the belt and open, but when they did what they found inside was incredible. There were four large coins, made of solid gold the size of a dinner plate and over an inch thick, with some kind of inscriptions in symbols of an alphabet none of them recognised. It also had the face of a bearded man on one side, and two crossed double-headed axes on the reverse side. Each coin weighed nearly 20 kilograms. They placed two in the sack, leaving the other two near a large olive tree a little way from the dead giant, and took turns carrying it while slowly making their way back to the Valenti compound with all their weapons. They arrived just as dusk was settling in. None of them touched the dead polyp-looking thing outside the front door and were let in only after some questions from Elizabeth and Jane.

Douglas had arrived too, along with two officers from the Rimini base, in order for a full debriefing of what had happened with the giants, as well as to take away the doppelganger, or shapeshifter, or whatever it was that Jane had dispatched.

It would take a few hours until they retired for the evening.

6

In the Val d'Aosta region of Italy, Captain De Dominicis was cursing his bad luck, the demons from Hell that were coming through the portal, the six tac-nukes it had required to close it, the fact that he was not even a Piedmontese, being from Abruzzo, and he didn't want to be in this Godforsaken shithole, in the snow, part of the last battalion that survived the ongoing onslaught of giants, dinosaur-like creatures, zombies, ghoul-like creatures, giant insects of all kinds, and on, and on, and on, in this endless nightmare that had become his life.

But he steeled himself with a stream of curses under his breath, thinking of the many young and scared soldiers under his command that looked to him for leadership. He was the most senior surviving officer and he had kept most of his company, composed of 125 men originally, alive. In the thick of battle with the endless stream of abominations his battalion had faced, De Dominicis had seen that the creatures tended to head towards the lower ground, the valleys and the farmlands below the alps, and since his battalion was getting slaughtered, he had ordered his men to fall back in a fighting retreat to higher ground. They had gradually managed to remove themselves from the fighting as it died down. The other six companies that had formed the battalion he belonged to were essentially destroyed. A few shell-shocked survivors ambled about several hundred metres below their position. They were also low on ammo, but as they continued to observe the land below, they saw that finally, the stream of supernatural creatures was starting to dwindle, and likely would be reduced to nothing overnight. It was freezing cold up here and they were not equipped to make a night of it so high up in the mountains, so he gave the order to start heading back down after ensuring every man had a loaded gun with him.

The sun would not stay up much longer and fighting at night with some of these things was the last thing De Dominicis wanted to be doing. On his paper map he saw there was a remote village about five kilometres away, on the other side of the small valley below them. Information on it was scant, but it was old, dating back to medieval times, so De Dominicis thought it should have some kind of keep or maybe even fortifications. He doubted that it had survived the passage of so many monsters, but they should be able to clear it out and take it over for security and a place to sleep that could be defended.

His men need a morale boost. He gathered them around and spoke at a normal level of voice. He didn't want to shout and make more noise than was necessary, and in any case the silence from his men was total. They all desperately hoped he would deliver them good news. *Short and to the point.* He thought.

"Men, there is a village about five kilometres away across this valley. That is where we will go. I am going to tell you all something important now. Please pay attention."

The men had all huddled close to each other, both for warmth and to avoid their captain having to shout. Their combined body heat was starting to clear patches of snow near them.

"Our battalion has been destroyed. On the way to this village we will gather any survivors and do our best to care for them. Communication with main command has been lost too. Our radio doesn't pick up anything. But this is the important part: We need to survive. You all need to survive. This is no longer about following orders, but just about getting you home alive and safe."

He looked into the faces looking up at him. A few were injured, many looked shell-shocked, a few were silently crying into their hands, trying to stifle their sobs. *They are all so young. Use it!*

"You are all young. And I want you all to get back to your families, your girlfriends and whatever else makes it worth living for you." He let that sink in for a few seconds.

"But there is only one way we can do this, and that is if we start to act like a coherent unit hellbent on outliving everything this shitty place has vomited out from the guts of Hell."

He saw the defeat in their eyes. The lack of hope.

"We are not fighting for any government anymore. Or taking any orders from higher ups anymore. But you will still need to take orders from me until we are back home and safe. If that's not acceptable to you, leave right now."

He waited two full minutes and then asked if there was anyone who did not want to obey any orders he might give. He also reassured the men that if the answer was "yes," nothing bad will happen to such people. No punishment, of any kind, no repercussions.

Not a single man got up.

"Be careful now, if you want to leave, right now, you can. And if we make it back to base, I will say you are MIA, Missing in Action, not AWOL."

No one moved.

"But if you stay, you agree to follow my orders and to do your very best to protect every man in this battalion."

He pointed to a corporal he knew.

"Tiramino, count how many of us there are, and how many wounded."

"Yes sir." Corporal Tiramino got up and started walking between the men, tapping them on the shoulder as he walked past them and counting silently in his head.

"We are fighting for each other now. And our families, and the families of your fellow soldiers here with you. Protect each other so we can all get back home to our loved ones."

The light in their eyes had almost come back on, thought De Dominicis.

"And we are no longer soldiers in the Italian Army. We are just men. Brothers in arms, who want to go back to our homes. Is that okay with you guys?"

There was a unanimous "Yes, Sir!" that was both spontaneous and quickly muted a little, as people shushed each other after the shout.

"So, we need a new name, Company. Talk among yourselves in groups of five and elect a speaker and I will ask you your suggestions in five minutes." As the men started talking, De Dominicis waited for corporal Tiramino to get back to him, which he did shortly thereafter.

"There are ninety-nine of us, including you, sir. Seventeen wounded, three quite badly who will need to be helped or carried."

"Thank you, Tiramino."

Tiramino shrugged, as if to say *it's nothing*, before doing a half-hearted salute and saying, "Duty, sir."

The twenty suggestions were voted on by making two groups of five agree on taking on only one of the names of the two teams, and then the process was repeated. Once they only had five names left De Dominicis said it would be put to a vote with his vote breaking any ties, but one of the companies surrendered their name in favour of one of the others so it came down to only four names.

The votes were as follows:

Yeti — 27

White Knights — 15

Black Luck Company — 28

Nec Spe Nec Metu — 28

Not wanting to upset the men De Dominicis said that since both Yeti and White Knights had lost, those soldiers should pick between one of the two remaining names. And wouldn't you know it, they had an even split, with 49 soldiers on each side.

They wanted De Dominicis to choose. He didn't want to, as it would tend to upset half his company.

"Who has the most wounded, each side, if you are wounded raise your hand."

Nec Spe Nec Metu the Latin phrase for *Without Hope, Without Fear,* had more wounded. It would work out perfectly thought De Dominicis.

"Alright then. We will call ourselves the Black Luck Company, and our motto will be Nec Spe, Nec Metu."

The men were quiet for a second or two, then he saw the smiles start to appear and a few subdued hurrahs and fists in the air.

It was a simple thing. A little ritual, but it had worked. He had given the men a new sense of hope, a purpose, and a new, ritualised name that pretty much embodied how he felt: *Shitty luck, but a steel-minded determination to not die as a result of these fucking Hell-creatures,* he thought.

They made make-shift stretchers for the three wounded men and started to head down into the valley where they could still see a few scattered soldiers, some wounded wretches dragging themselves along. A giant or two trudging through the snow with large wolves that roamed the small valley alongside them, and from time to time attacked one of the few survivors below. One man in particular seemed to have the will to stay alive. He had shot one of the large wolves with his underpowered military issue 5.56mm weapon, but it had dropped. They could hear the reports, he had it on single semi-automatic fire, and they could even see tiny flashes from the rifle as he knelt and took aim at the next wolf charging him. He fired quickly four, five shots. The wolf fell face first in the snow and was trying to get up. The soldier stood, ran to the wolf and when he was only a couple of metres from it fired into its head as the wolf tried to raise it toward him.

The noise had attracted one of the two giants they could see, who had started to walk in the snow, almost waist high for the lone soldier, who was now using the large wolf's body as a sort of sandbag. He appeared to be reloading or fidgeting with his rifle. The whole of Black Luck Company was looking at the spectacle below them, playing out crystal clear if too far for them to help the man, he must be about a kilometre or more away, and they too only had assault rifles in 5.56mm. Even if they reached the giant, the ammunition at that distance would hardly trouble the creature.

The giant started to take faster and larger steps towards the fallen wolf and the man behind its body. The giant was lunging forward in a loping, long stride, its blue-tinged exposed arms and face adding to the terrifying sense of the surreal these creatures emanated. The man just lay half on the wolf, using it as a rest for his rifle and seemed to be waiting. When the giant was so close that the men thought the soldier must be out of ammo —because he had not fired— a single shot rang out, and the giant clapped his left hand to its face. Another shot. And the other hand went to the other eye of the giant. Then the man stood up, jumped over the wolf, towards the giant, standing now, aimed and fired a rapid succession of shots. They must have been aimed at the giant's groin because the creature bent down over itself even as it stepped forward twice, coming really close to the man now.

The soldier dropped the rifle in the snow, did something with his hands and threw something just under the head of the giant, who was half-bent over, then the man picked up his rifle, hopped back over the wolf and lay down in the snow.

The grenade he had thrown went off not five metres from the giant's face, and this made the creature jerk upright, overbalance and fall backwards, even as it let out a guttural scream of pain and frustration. The soldier had stood up and was now running, but at an oblique angle, not directly away from the giant but towards a rise that would hide him from the other giant that was further away and coming from the same direction from which the now badly wounded one had come.

The giant lying on its back was roaring in pain and kicking and rolling around in the snow. The other giant, carrying a spear, trotted up to it, and the lone soldier lay down still in the snow, having barely made it to the ridge, so that he was hidden from the creature; assuming it hadn't already seen him. From were De Dominicis and his soldiers were, it was hard to tell.

When the second giant reached the downed one, who was still raging and screaming, as well as kicking up a flurry of snow and ice that was impressive in its width and breath, it knelt down, and seemed to bark some orders to the wounded one, who tried to be still but still twisted and turned a bit but had removed its hands from its face.

The giant with the spear stood, turned its spear point down, lifted it with both hands and skewered the wounded giant through the neck. Some of the soldiers laughed.

The blue-skinned giant, frost in its beard and the giant spear dripping black fluid, started to make its way towards where the lone soldier had run.

No. Thought De Dominicis. He lifted his rifle and fired three rounds, aiming a full giant and half-length above the one walking in the valley below them. They had all shared ammunition. They didn't have any to spare. They were down to five rounds per man. And De Dominicis had just fired three at the giant, pointlessly.

The monstrous creature had stopped and turned to look in their direction though, and De Dominicis could not help himself; he shouted:

"Charge! Black Company, Charge that fucker! We are not going to let it kill one of our boys! Charge!" He had been towards the back of the march and now he ran, a little clumsily in the deep snow, with his legs lifting high for each step, he was not a big man, but he ran as hard as he could and he was shouting at the top of his voice. The men, first surprised, then amused, and finally taken in by their Captain's absurd and crazy notion, laughed and began to join in, screaming and whooping as they started to run with him.

"Save your ammo, and do what that boy did. Aim for the eyes when we can see them clearly. Let's get that blue fucker! Go, Go, Go! Charge! Charge!"

The giant below looked up at the mountainside and the dozens of ant-like humans running at him. *Firing their little weapons, they were still dangerous. Thigor had been blinded and would have become useless as the result of one of those insects. He should be avenged.* He started to sweep his spear into the snow.

"Run boys, run! He's looking for rocks to throw at us! Run, get close!"

By the time the Black company had reached half the distance between them and the giant named Thurind, the creature had ripped a boulder out of the snow-covered ground, and hurled it at them.

"Incoming!" Shouted De Dominicis.

The throw was accurate and landed in the middle of the troops, but most had seen it coming and moved out of the way. No one was hit directly, but two men took rocky shrapnel from the resulting shards created by the impact. One was now another serious case, the other had a broken leg.

Black company continued to advance, but a few of the soldiers dropped to one knee and started to take aim, then fired one round. About a dozen such single shots rang out, and the giant seemed to flinch several times, and even dropped his giant spear at one point. *The boys are all aiming for its head,* thought De Dominicis, proudly. *That's good. They are not afraid anymore, they are pissed off, like me. That's very good,* he thought, bloody-mindedly and with the hint of an angry smirk on his face. *We are going to kill, you, you giant bastard!*

The Black Luck Company carried on running towards the giant, with some of the best riflemen periodically dropping to one knee and firing a single round, while the ones that had done so previously ran to catch up. They started to work together in unison, without De Dominicis having had to say anything. They all wanted to kill that giant too. It looked in the snow for another boulder, then seemed to start to worry and gathered up only a handful of rocks and flung it at the charging group of men, but they were too spaced out, and luckily none were hit by the handful of fist sized rocks that had been flung at them at close to pistol-round velocity. The men were now all running at it and as they hit a patch of clearer ground had sped up and were now within three hundred metres. The giant, was looking visibly worried now, judging from its hesitant movements. De Dominicis sensed it and dropped to one knee, shouting an order:

"Fire at its face, it's going to run!"

Several men followed his example as De Dominicis fired his last two rounds. The Giant flung an arm up over its eyes, then did in fact turn and start to run directly away from them back towards were the lone soldier had laid down, though in all the commotion no one had kept track of where that man was now.

The giant only made it half-way back towards where the lone soldier had originally hidden, behind the small rise there, with the reports of aimed rounds chasing him as the sting of the little bullets peppered his back, then a single report from the valley saw the giant howl, and reach one hand up to its face as it turned its head skywards, arching its back. That lone soldier must have run up closer to the giant while it had been focussing on the Black Luck Company, and was now close enough to have shot it in its left eye.

The giant recovered, lifting it spear, another report, but the giant flung the spear without flinching, even though its left hand remained on its face, covering the left eye.

De Dominicis could not see the soldier. The giant's body was obstructing the view, but he stood up and started running towards the giant as fast as he could, waving his right arm as he went, and shouting "Charge! Charge! Black Company, charge!"

He'd dropped the word *Luck* from the name for expediency, and later, some of the men would too; it was implied after all.

The giant had flung its right arm up to protect its remaining good eye and rushed forward, probably intending to stomp the lone soldier into the ground. Single rapid-fire shots rang out from the valley, but now the whole of the Black Luck Company —except for the wounded and those tending to them— was running towards the giant. They were still a couple hundred meters or so from the creature.

The giant flinched at each report and screamed in a rage as it rushed forward one way then the other, stomping the ground partially blind, and then De Dominicis saw it. The lone soldier was standing, firing at the giant's face judging from the angle of his rifle. The creature was now maybe only a dozen metres from the soldier. The man was trying to move and shoot at the same time, trying to get past the giant so it would have to turn to face the Black Company in order to get him, but the giant was also trying to cut him off while guessing more or less where the man was, as it could only take glances for fear of having its other eye shot out. And the soldier in the meantime harassed the giant with what must have been accurate fire to its face since it flinched after every report. De Dominicis could see the soldier was unlikely to make it without some luck and some help.

"Shoot! Shoot at its face! Shoot!" he shouted to his men while he continued running. A small part of his brain was wondering what the hell he would do if he got there. He was out of rifle ammo, and he doubted his Beretta service pistol would do anything to the giant, but he also knew if he stopped running, so would his men. Some did anyway as he started to hear intermittent reports from behind him. They were briefly spaced out and coming from different spots behind him, which meant his men were continuing to co-ordinate to conserve ammo and act intelligently. The giant ahead of him started to twitch more and the arm it was keeping up over its eyes started to move more erratically. Its left hand too was no longer holding his broken eye, and it too was erratically trying to prevent the bullets from landing on its head mostly. De Dominicis was looking at the lone soldier, so close to the giant, he had stopped moving and was just waiting with his rifle raised high towards the creature's face.

Cold blooded dude, thought De Dominicis, *he's biding his time to get the right shot off at the giant,* and just as he thought that, the man fired and the giant's head snapped backwards, a howl of raging pain roared out of its skyward-turned mouth, that echoed in the mountain valleys with a terror-inducing consequence. The soldier had hit its other eye. The man immediately turned and ran at an angle, away from the giant and curving towards the oncoming Black Company.

The men who could run had now all started to run towards the giant again, sensing it was in trouble, like a small and vengeful school of land-piranhas, they were closing in for the kill. The giant raged a bit more then, having lost its orientation and being blind, it had started to wander towards the Black Company, coming closer to them even as they ran. None of them slowed down or started shooting, as a group, they had all realised that as soon as they would the giant would turn and run in the opposite direction, and they didn't want it to get away. They only stopped once they were only about fifty metres away from it, and without shouting or making noise, one of the corporals had used hand signals to wave them all down and kneel and point their rifles at the thing. It was still holding its arms over its face, so when about fifty men had lined up, the corporal pointed to his own throat and groin, as these would be the targets to shoot for. He then pulled out a grenade and pointed to five of the men closest to him that had some left, and he indicated they should get ready with grenades too, though a fifty-metre throw was an optimistic one at best. Then he raised his arm and brought it down fast, firing-squad style. De Dominicis had come up behind the kneeling men, observing and proud of his men executing this without one word from him.

They all fired in almost perfect unison and De Dominicis saw an expanding spatter of black splotches appear on the giant's neck and straw-coloured beard. It gurgled in sudden shock, flailed about for a while, then, as a second volley of shots hit it, it fell face first in the snow. It was still groaning and gurgling for a bit as the lone soldier made his way towards the men, looping carefully around the giant at a safe distance. By the time he got to De Dominicis the giant had stopped moving.

"Welcome soldier," said De Dominicis greeting the man, who had that thousand-yard stare of men who should have been by all rights shell-shocked, but kept fighting because they knew no other way.

Tiramino was the corporal who had taken charge and was standing next to him, and he too greeted the man.

"Welcome, Hundred."

De Dominicis looked at Tiramino, an unspoken question on his arched brow. Tiramino looked at his Captain a little sheepishly, and said, "Eh, we are one hundred now, and he deserves a nickname, sir."

De Dominicis knew that as with all soldiers, each man eventually acquired a nickname, given to him by his brothers in arms. Often not very flattering ones. He didn't say anything, but turned back to the man.

"What's your name soldier?"

"Giuseppe D'Amaso." The man paused a few seconds, before he remembered to add *sir* to the reply.

"Welcome D'Amaso, I see from your insignia you were part of our original battalion. You wounded?" The man's coat was slashed open but De Dominicis could not see any blood.

D'Amaso shook his head then looked at the slashed coat and back to De Dominicis, "No sir, this was the spear he threw at me. I was lucky, managed to move a bit and he just missed me."

De Dominicis nodded and the soldier spoke again.

"Sir, I am out of ammo. That last shot I fired at its eye was my last round."

The man looked exhausted and his face had a day or two's growth of facial hair on it. His eyes still spoke of the horrors he had seen, but De Dominicis knew this man would be alright. He was still thinking. Still paying attention to what mattered. He nodded to him and started to explain what their new mission was now, the little village a few kilometres away, and basic survival. He'd also asked Tiramino to gather all the men, including the wounded ones, and give a full count of remaining weaponry. He also instructed a dozen men to go and pick over the bodies of fallen soldiers they could find nearby and return with any ammunition or service pistols they found. He promoted Tiramino to Sargent-Major, and D'Amaso to Sargent of special operations on the spot.

By the time they had re-grouped there were a hundred of them, though a handful had to be helped or carried in makeshift stretchers, two of which had been made by cutting up the spear of the giant, and stretching and tying some of its furs across the two poles. The men were reduced to a mere three rounds each even after having scavenged ammunition from the dead.

They still had almost four kilometres to go and they would reach the village only when it was going to have started to get dark. De Dominicis tasked D'Amaso and a dozen of his fittest men to go ahead and try and secure the village. They had given each man in this team a full ten rounds each, resulting in everyone else having only two rounds left. De Dominicis had none left and neither did

Tiramino, but they both had service pistols with two full magazines, as did D'Amaso, having received one of the recovered pistols from some unfortunate officer.

The forward team led by D'Amaso was travelling very light and went off at a very brisk page. They meant to get there before dark, which meant they needed to move quickly.

7

In the depth of the Swiss underground complex where the self-styled "Princes of Hell" gathered, an emergency session had been called.

Seated in each of the thrones placed at vertices of the six-pointed star made of solid gold lines embedded in the obsidian-dark floor of the huge chamber, sat one of the Princes.

Prince Abeleth, the eldest man there was speaking now.

"They were able to block the openings much faster than we expected. It has been disappointing, although the portals in South America and Australia remain open for now, it will not be long before they close those too."

The other hooded men remained silent, waiting for Prince Abeleth to continue.

"One unexpected positive result is that in the shutting them down a shockwave of apparitions was also produced, so our efforts have had a good impact anyway, but we must organise ourselves for a future event, and it would be prudent to eliminate the source of this… interference."

Prince Orath, Master of Asia spoke.

"Prince Abeleth, do we know who is responsible?"

"We do. A man called Douglas Jones."

"Do we have resources nearby to take care of him?" asked Prince Laduvim, Master of Europe.

"We have several emissaries in the overall region. It will take a few days for them to… well… we are not yet sure to what extent the creatures from beyond can be controlled yet, are we?" Prince Abeleth laughed, though due to his advanced age it sounded more like the dry rasping of a man dying of tuberculosis.

"It will be a good opportunity to see if the predicted rituals and precautions for the direction of the undead work as we envision," said Prince Laduvim.

"Indeed," responded Prince Kaarik, Master of South America.

"They shut down the portal in Chad yesterday, though not without massive loss of life," smiled Prince Jakkiry, Master of Africa. "How long before they shut down the portal in Australia, do you think, Prince Abeleth?"

"A few days at most, which should be enough to reduce the population to a mere fraction in due course. And Africa is already well on the path. Their resources were always minimal and even the remnants from three years ago have continued to cause population reduction and general mayhem, with little to slow them down," replied Prince Abeleth.

"It may be shut down sooner than we imagine, Princes," it was Prince Rathienor, Master of Australia, "I just had word shortly before this meeting that a Chinese aircraft carrier was in range. They should be launching nuclear warheads as we speak. I assume the American one heading to Chile will also be nearly in position soon enough."

There was silence for a long minute, before Prince Abeleth spoke up again.

"We have been patient for a long time, and we must continue to exercise patience still. In the last three years we have reduced the world's population by a little more than half. This new influx of planar beings will reduce it further, though it may take some time, and the beauty of it is that under these conditions, people are less likely to reproduce." He took a pause to catch his breath before continuing.

"In the meantime, we must identify groups and individuals that pose any sort of obstacle and begin using our chosen troop leaders to begin to organise the various creatures into operational castes.

These will then be sent to destroy those who would stand in our way or slow the process down."

"The projections are that over the next few years the human population will be reduced to less than a billion. So, we will still have work to do, but if the current studies yield any useful pathogen or other avenues, we may well get to our target of something under half a billion servants, in the next couple of years."

There were a few further discussions on various aspects of their Satanic agenda that were discussed, but the final outcome of the meeting was that the next pressing matter was the organisation of death squads of supernatural beings to be organised to destroy Douglas Jones and his associates; preferably with the capture of any children, which would then be used in the usual rituals before being consumed while still partially alive, as was the custom for these men.

8

Taro Valenti woke with a start, and next to him, his wife Jane was also tossing around and saying "No!" though clearly, she was not really awake. His heart still pounding, Taro grabbed her arm, called out to her, "Jane. Jane, wake up!" gently shaking her, while at the same time he also tried to look around in the almost pitch-dark bedroom. He couldn't see anything, but the nightmare he had had was still present in his nervous system and he wanted to make sure there was no other presence in his bedroom besides his wife.

"Jane," he patted her gently on the cheek, "wake up darling, wake up."

Jane scrunched her eyes half-open, then sat up, afraid suddenly, "What? What is it?" She reached out and smashed the switch for her bedside lamp on.

Taro flinched; his eyes almost closed at the sudden intrusion of light in his pupils.

"You were having a bad dream. Me too."

"Yeah... no shit. I dreamt I shot you and an octopus with a beak like an owl was eating Marco and Alina."

"Well, octopi do have beaks..." said Taro.

"Yeah," said Jane with sarcasm dripping from her voice like molasses, "that's the *important* part of the dream. Good thing I got *that* detail right eh?"

Taro had been trying to distract her, and it worked, but her new target was not really what he had meant to achieve.

"Well, I had the same dream, pretty much. You were shooting me in the face and another me that wasn't me, with evil eyes, just behind you, was smiling as you did it. The blast of buckshot to my face woke me up with a start."

"Fuck," she said sounding tired and defeated, "I hate this new world. All these fucking monsters…"

"Aw babe, come on, how many times do you get the satisfaction of shooting your husband in the face and not suffer the consequences eh?" Taro was trying to lighten the mood. He worried about Jane getting too stressed by all the terrifying insanity they had been dealing with on an almost daily basis since that first werewolf had appeared three years earlier.

Jane leaned into him, hugging him and putting her head against his chest even as they were sitting in bed.

"Don't even joke. I didn't say anything, but it was horrible, Taro. It's messed with my head a lot."

"Well, that's probably a good thing. I wouldn't want you getting used to shooting me in the face as a general habit."

She snorted a little, but she was holding him tight. He kissed the top of her head as he held her with one arm too.

After a little while he spoke again.

"Look babe, I know it's hard, but… in a way, it's kind of cool. It beats all the paperwork, and shitty modified food, and chemtrails, and bureaucratic little Nazis trying to rule every aspect of our lives, and digital fake money, and all those millions of fake religions all trying to convince you of their lies, and so on. Honestly, sure it's more dangerous, but it's also simpler, more honest and… more… alive, I guess."

"I know, I know," she said a little despondently, this was not the first time they had this type of conversation.

"But I just… sometimes I would like to just wear a nice sundress, go to a spa, drink my vanilla latte while I get my nails done, and have the kids play around in a normal playground. Instead of always feeling like a dirt farmer from the eighteenth century, but with monsters, and my kids having to learn hand-signals to become fucking commandos, so they might not get eaten by some poisonous demon or a shape-shifting other version of me or you!"

"Well, there is that…" replied Taro, "but come on, what kind of boring ass chick-flick kind of film would that be?"

"I'd like a bit of bored chick-flick romance right now, really," she said sadly.

"Well… I don't have the long, flowing locks of a romance novel cover model, darling, but here I am…" He moved her back a little and kissed her gently.

"Yeah," she said moving back a little after the kiss, "and your idea of romance is telling me the detailed breakdown of the latest gun Douglas can get you from the American armoury."

"Oh, woman! You know how to get me all excited when you start talking that way, come here!" He kissed her again and she was smiling a little now.

ȣ•ȣ

"But why can't I have a piece of it? For my experiments! And *you* got me the microscope, dad!"

They were all sitting at breakfast, and Scarlet was complaining because Taro had said no to her getting a piece of the doppelganger that Jane had shot the day before.

"Look, they have already taken it away and some of those things will kill you on contact. Remember the Hellfrog I told you about. Douglas' friend was killed because he thought he could just touch it like a normal frog." Taro was trying to be patient with Scarlet, but she had been going on about this for several minutes already.

"Well that was foolish of him, it doesn't even look like a normal frog," she said scowling a little.

"Precisely, and you want to do "experiments" with a piece of a creature that for all you know will turn to poisonous gas the minute you add any other element to it and kill us all. Or maybe turn *you* into one of them," said Taro.

"Cooool!" She said right away, totally avoiding Taro's intended point, "that way I could pretend to be Marco, or Alina, or even Anna or Arianna, and you guys would be so confused!" She laughed.

"No!" Said Alina forcefully, "I would shoot you! Like mommy did to the not-daddy!"

Well this has taken a bad turn, thought Taro, as he often did when his children started to go off at random tangents.

"No one is shooting anyone of us!" Said Jane, clearly irritated.

"Dad," said Marco sitting on Taro's right, "But... but... if Scarlet turned into one of those double-gangsters, could we freeze her, put her in the big freezer and so she can't eat us, but she's still alive? But frozen."

Taro just looked at his son stupefied, "How... how does that thought even get into your head son?"

"You wouldn't be able to freeze me! I would turn you into an octopus double-gangster too!" Said Scarlet from the end of the table where she was sitting opposite Taro.

"No one is becoming an octopus either! Now shut up and eat your breakfast, all of you!" Jane was clearly getting stressed.

Anna and Arianna had kept quiet throughout, both eating their porridge while looking at each other across the table and smiling and making "ooohh, and oooops," kind of faces, wanting to avoid the trouble their siblings seemed to be getting into with their parents, but still having fun about it.

The table was suddenly quiet for a few seconds, then Marco's soft voice was heard:

"But dad, if you froze a Scarlet-Octopus double-gangster, would she still be alive when you defrost her?"

Taro couldn't help it. He burst out laughing. Between the mispronunciation of doppelganger Marco had come up with, and the image of a shape-shifting octopus-like Scarlett with a fedora and a tommy gun that came to his mind, at the absurd question, it was unavoidable. Marco laughed too and so did everyone else.

Jane looked at Taro, before he noticed her doing so, and in that half-second or so before he turned, she saw him at ease, *laughing with our children,* she thought, *all of them happy, and this man somehow had made it so that despite everything we are all here, and alive, and better prepared for this insane world than most of everyone else on the planet.* She not often had the thought consciously, even though she felt the emotion; *God, I do love him so. Thank you, for him.*

Later that day, he had met with Douglas and they had discussed several issues, one of which was the reply from the Russians that the Australian portal had been closed by the Chinese aircraft carrier, and they had managed to keep the shockwave to the small radius, and the Chilean portal should be within range of nuclear armed stealth bombers later that day.

The other news from the Russians was that they had identified a half-dozen locations that could house at least some of the Davos Satanists, as Douglas referred to them generally, but all of those locations were deep underground and likely safe from hypersonic nuclear ICBM attacks, and worse, they formed part of large complexes that housed hundreds of thousands of civilians too. They explained that they were busy putting together some extraction teams but that they would expect heavy resistance and entering into fortified nuclear bunkers was not going to be an easy thing no matter how it was approached. And in any case, there was no certainty as to even exactly who all of the players were, much less where they were exactly.

It was very frustrating. The people who had resulted in the death of over half the planet's population were still mostly unknown and their crime continued to go unpunished. Some of their wealthier and better-known puppet-masters had been summarily executed by angry mobs. One in particular had had a bunker in Hawaii, and the people there had mostly survived with little effect, thanks to being on an island that had only one small portal on it. The islanders eventually either figured out or assumed the billionaire was involved somehow. They had first dug up and blasted all around the entrances and air-vents they could find with mining explosives, then they got cement truck after cement truck to pour concrete over the craters and damaged parts of the complex. *He had wanted to be an emperor over us,* they had said, *let him be buried alive in his own giant tomb.* With no way to cycle the air, everyone inside would eventually suffocate, even if they had carbon scrubbers, which no one could say if they did or not. Almost two years later, the bunker had an opening blasted into it, and the remains of the tech billionaire and his whole family and retinue of hangers on was found. They had all expired from suffocation.

"We need to get these assholes," said Douglas, "They are not going to stop until they have destroyed the whole planet, otherwise."

"I still don't get their big-picture agenda. How do they plan to get rid of all the critters after they reduce us down to whatever the old exploded Georgia guide-stones said; half-a billion, was it?" asked Taro.

"Yeah. Who knows, they are insane, or maybe…" an idea came to Douglas for the first time, "…maybe they have a way to phase them all back to wherever they came from. Some reversing of the process that targets these creatures that came through the portal.

Maybe by their weird DNA. Or some other mechanism…" Douglas trailed off. The path his thoughts were taking became obvious to Taro too.

"So, you think maybe there is a way to send them all back at once?" he asked Douglas.

"No idea yet, and if there is, I can't think of how; not off the top of my head, but it may be a thing to look into."

"Do you have the men to do it?"

"Cooper is coming along nicely, and he's asked me if he can get his fiancée to help too. She has a good brain on her, they could start statistical analyses on the samples we have and see if anything comes of it. I'll put a protocol together later today."

Taro noticed Douglas had a new vigour in him as a result of this most recent idea. *A good thing,* he thought. *Douglas needs a few more wins.* The man was too hard on himself, but Taro understood that way of being too.

"Good," replied Taro, "in the meantime, we need to try and prepare our village and the nearby areas for more of those giants. I'm, going to see Alessandro. Maybe try and put together some kind of team for the Swiss in the meantime?"

"I'll try, but we are far from Switzerland, and probably way under-gunned for it. But sure. I'll start some kind of roster." Douglas had not looked hopeful.

Alessandro Arfelli was one of those few who, like Taro and Douglas, had opted to live outside the protection of the village walls. A successful artisan who worked with metal before the portals appeared, he was well equipped to do so. He had built many of Monte Castello's defences, including metal portcullises, retractable metal spikes up the walls of the village and around it to prevent scaling, pit traps, and so on.

Because he had chosen to live outside the walls, he too was referred to as one of the "crazies". At least, that was the name given to those who opted to survive outside the walls with their families. Alessandro had two daughters; both had taken his classical good looks as well as those of their equally beautiful mother Silvia. Elisa was thirteen, and Elena fourteen. The sisters were close in both age and sisterly conspiratorial loyalty. Pretty, smart, and having learnt a lot from their father about metal-work and general defence structures made of metal, it was not unusual to see them kitted out in a welder's mask helping their father, with a handgun strapped to their leg like some young lady adventurers from out of a dystopian manga film. Which wasn't far from what they were living in anyway, thought Taro as he approached their home. Alessandro had set up various detectors and was waiting for him at the compound's gate by the time he got close.

After greeting each other and exchanging pleasantries, and after Taro had explained about the giants, they had retired to Alessandro's home workshop.

Laid out on a large table was a topographic map of the entire area and Alessandro started to discuss with Taro where they could build large, metal, caltrop-style area denial barriers. Mostly as a similar deterrent to what soldiers in the Second World War had found on the beaches in Normandy. Except made for humanoids that were some ten metres in height, or basically the height of a four-story building. It would take time and would require all the backhoes and tractors the village could muster. Alessandro had a very large tractor/backhoe/tank thing he had put together himself. It was huge, mostly painted orange and his daughters called it Arturo, which Taro thought was very incongruent since it made killdozer look like a scaled-up toy. Arturo seemed far too an innocuous name for it.

Both Elisa and Elena had made suggestions too for the village defences, listening and not interrupting unnecessarily. The girls clearly had minds that functioned well from a strategic point of view. They pointed out ravines and deep valleys that would make good kill zones, and other areas that would be easy to defend. Taro found himself hoping his son Marco was a little older; he could do worse than finding a young woman like one of these two when he got a bit older. As things stood, it was not too early to try and see which young girl might end up being a decent daughter-in-law some years down the line. Taro realised, as he had these fleeting thoughts, that perhaps human beings naturally thought in these tribal and quasi-feudal ways, and it had only been the artificial absurdities of the world before the monsters that had masked them. *Or maybe I'm just a primitive throwback to a few centuries ago.* He smiled to himself, thinking how that would undoubtedly be Jane's view if he ever voiced such thoughts to her.

Silvia had brought them snacks and drinks while they looked at the best places to try and protect, as well as how to funnel any eventual giants that might come their way. Taro hoped it would not be a horde, but only a few at most, because otherwise they were all doomed. The few tanks and half-tracks that were available from any military left nearby would be deployed around the major arteries and roads that still worked. Monte Castello was very defensible, but not particularly important strategically, even if it had been the site of a difficult battle in the Second World War.

Elena had suggested a pair of drones be put up to fly around the village perimeter at high altitude with constant manning around the clock as an early warning system. Elisa said she would do no more than four hour shifts though. Not out of laziness but because she had learnt that was about the limit before attention dropped off. The girls took it upon themselves to put together a team of young people from the village school they attended. They would need probably a dozen people and at least four drones to keep the drones charged, in the air, and useful. After they had left, Taro told Alessandro he was impressed with the girls' attitude.

"Children adapt faster than us," said Alessandro simply.

"They do," agreed Taro.

"All we can do is give them our experience in those things we are good at." Alessandro was watching the girls retreating to the main house with their mother as he and Taro finished up.

"And give them a killer instinct," said Taro.

"Like I said, whatever we are good at. I'll stick to metalwork." Alessandro was smiling. Taro had given some basic training to several people in the village when it came to dealing with the various creatures, and having been the first guy who had figured out how to kill the more difficult monsters like werewolves and vampires, who were not affected by normal weapons, he had gained a slight reputation.

He was never sure what it was really, for at least a year, but he noted people seemed a little tense around him and rarely disagreed openly with him. When he had brought it up to Jane eventually, she had looked at him as if he were retarded.

"It's fear, darling! They are scared of a guy who just instinctively comes up with a way to kill werewolves on the spot out of the blue."

"Ummm, you mean, kindly respect, surely. For my wisdom and… gentlemanly ways…"

She had laughed. "Babe, you're pretty big, you have a scary kind of face, you're not shy about correcting people if they are not being careful, and you shoot first and don't even bother with questions, trust me, people are nervous around you."

"Wha-aat? I'm just killing monsters, it's not like I rape and pillage the villagers!" He had said, a little incredulous that she might have a point. *Surely people are not actually scared of me?*

"That's why they tolerate you dear. It's how they know you're on our side."

He hadn't replied, but the thought had bothered him a little. *I'm a nice guy, what's wrong with people*! At least Alessandro was just poking fun at him. *Probably*, he thought.

It was nightfall before Taro headed back home and he knew Jane would be worried, as she always did when he was walking home at night from somewhere. In fairness, Taro was alert and worried himself, but he was armed with his shotgun and the custom-made Colt Dragoon; and Alessandro had driven him most of the way to his home before dropping him off. The loss of the Humvee was a pain. He doubted he'd get another one anytime soon.

9

Samuele Schwartz was the highest Freemason of the local chapter. The small black orb he held in his hand was able to keep the shades at bay in his home Temple's summoning room.

Six hooded vampires in ragged clothes, stood around him. Each at the apex of one of the points of the star traced in the floor in gold that Schwartz stood in the centre of. The creatures had unnaturally pale and not quite human limbs, tipped with pointed, three-inch long nails so black that they seemed to absorb any light directly out of the aether. The hoods hid their bald and cadaverous-looking, gaunt, elongated faces, but not enough for Samuele's liking. Their pitch-black eyes without any white in them were unnerving, and any time their neurotic, almost insect-like movements resulted in any slight opening of their mouths, Samuele could see the hint of the maw of sharp, pointed teeth in jaws that could spread open far too wide for a human being.

That black orb was the only thing that prevented them from tearing him to pieces, he knew. And he was about to pass a similar orb to his number two lieutenant: Davide Soffiaforte.

Davide had been an architect before the portals. Not a very successful one, but whose ego certainly had palatial dimensions. He had joined the Freemasons to get better contracts. Not to mention access to the regular orgies that some of the rituals involved. His typically Italian wife had given him a single son, and was not particularly adventurous in bed, and Davide had never been a ladies' man, so the eventual passing into the higher levels of the organisation were overall exciting to him. And he didn't even mind the required humiliation rituals. So what if there was a little bisexuality required. He was finally getting bigger contracts. Then Hell had come to Earth, and he had been catapulted into positions of power he had only dreamt of. And now he was going to be given his first solo mission. Controlling six shades, as Samuele called them, though as far as Davide could tell they were a kind of vampire that could not be killed by normal weaponry.

Samuele was Davide's Master, of course, and as such Davide was bound to obey. He recalled only too well how Samuele had promoted him. A perverse sexual ritual in which Davide had been the "servant" of every member of the black robed men below him. Culminating with Samuele's final "marking" of Davide. After that harrowing night, however, he had become the third most powerful Freemason in the whole Emilia Romagna region. And the underlings were no longer permitted to make fun of his surname, which translated as *Blow (Soffia) Hard (Forte)*. It is what they had all laughed at him for even before the final unfortunate ritual, and he knew they still thought of him that way, but they couldn't voice it to his face anymore. And mutual contempt for everyone else was the way of Freemasonry after all. The strong and ambitious would rise above the others; by treading on their heads if need be, and doing whatever else was needed to achieve seniority. Davide would be in competition with the number one lieutenant, Andrea Cuccala who would be dispatched to his own mission shortly after this ritual was done. Davide's target was the Valenti family, Andrea would be going after the Jones'.

Davide intended to use his small time-advantage over Cuccala to the fullest extent. He had organised for some nearby villagers to attend a special Church ceremony —that would have no effect since the priest was a Novus Ordo one, and the host had been thoroughly desecrated— but the procession would take place directly between the temple and the Church at the hour Cuccala was due to leave with his team of six shades. It was likely he would be unable to control them, and they may attack the procession. The ensuing chaos would slow Cuccala down and with any luck even get him killed.

We'll see just how hard I blow, thought Davide, as he took one of the black orbs Samuele offered him, and began the chant in Latin.

Princeps Tenebrarum da mihi potestatem servis tuis ut devoret animas odiosarum animalium hominum

He then drank from the iron goblet Samuele handed to him, that contained the blood, semen, and urine of his master, and the crushed and desecrated host that had been procured by the fake priest. The foul taste in his mouth also made his stomach rumble but he would never reject the humours he had ingested; it would be a rejection of the power, and that he would not do.

Samuele handed him one orb, with the left hand, retaining the larger one in his right.

It was cold and heavy to the touch, and as soon as he wrapped his palm about it, Davide felt as if a slithering whisper had entered his head. He looked at the shades and thought of them lifting their arms to the moon far above the temple and hissing, and that is precisely what they did in unison. Their elongated and pale arms with the obsidian claws stretched high above their upturned pitch-black eyes, and the slithering, hissing sound of their open and terrifying maws went beyond the range of human ears. Dogs far in the distance barked as if going crazy, and a distant wolf-howl too was heard.

Davide was now the leader of a vampire pack. Six relentless, supernaturally fast, absurdly strong, killing machines at his command, who would not sleep or rest, and as long as he held the orb in contact with his skin, he would be safe from them and able to command them with his mind. Their only weakness was direct sunlight, Catholic Crosses held by people with true faith, and silver that had been blessed and imbibed with holy water by a true priest or bishop. Valenti might get one, maybe even two. But no man could best six of these Hellspawn at once. And that is precisely how Davide planned to use them. He would have the vampires hold Taro Valenti and make him watch while Davide used his woman and daughters. The boy would be saved for his master. Then he would have his family watch as the vampires tore Valenti apart in a frenzied feeding. Yes. All the humiliation, the ritual serving of the others, it was all worth it. Now he had more direct power than almost any human being that had ever lived on Earth in all its ages. And one day, he would build a giant castle, in the brutalist post-modernist style he favoured. He could already envision it: he would keep Valenti's skull on a wall in his throne room. After all, it was fitting, it was this mission that had given him command of six shades. He would also keep Valenti's wife as a slave chained to his throne. At least until he got bored of her.

He began to lead the shades out of the chamber, fully intending to begin the journey to the village of Monte Castello right away. They had to travel at night and on foot, and from the city of San Marino, inside the small nation of the same name, it was just over twenty kilometres in a straight line to Monte Castello; over valleys and rivers, the last of which the shades could not cross directly, one further weakness they had relating to running water in natural streams. So it would take probably until dawn to get close. They would attack tomorrow night if they managed to get close enough tonight. They would have to sleep rough in the forests nearby, and he had a backpack ready for it. He set off immediately, and saw Andrea entering the temple just as he left with his six servants in tow. He thought of making them scare Andrea, and they hissed at him before he could curb the thought, but Andrea seemed unfazed. *Damn his controlled demeanour*, thought Davide. But he consoled himself with what he had planned for a short while from now, and the fact he had an advantage, having set off first.

Now it was just the Valenti, and their flesh and pain and ravaging, that he would enjoy and luxuriate in immensely. That was all that mattered. The shades hissed softly in unison behind him, as his own thoughts ran through them too, as an extension of their unnatural bodily functions.

10

D'Amaso had reached the ancient little village when they still had maybe a half hour of sunlight left. It was clearly old and long-since abandoned. But a few of the structures still had functional roofs that meant they would be relatively easy to heat with a fire or some of their camp stoves, if they had enough of them. Three larger structures —that had probably been barns back in the day— were large enough to keep all hundred men between them if a little cramped.

D'Amaso had ordered the men to simply go in pairs through the village and to his relief, no weird critters had been discovered. He reasoned that perhaps they went after living things and this old deserted village was pretty much devoid of life.

He then tasked eight of the men to gather any old furniture, wooden beams, or anything that would burn and make three piles, one each near the entrance to each of the old barns. That way the men could sleep inside and a fire directly in front of each doorway would make it obvious if anything tried to get inside during the night.

When the rest of the Black Luck Company arrived, De Dominicis had more good news. They had found a functioning radio on the body of a dead soldier they had come across on the way here, and they had re-established a connection with the base near Turin. They had explained they were the last survivors, and the closing of the portal had meant that the flow of creatures from the mountains had eventually stopped.

Central command told them to return to base in the morning as there was more work needed to protect various villages and towns in the whole area since so many of the monsters had still managed to reach populated areas. There was distant machine-gun fire in the background whenever HQ came over the radio.

De Dominicis had explained his men were exhausted and out of ammo and wanted to protect their own families, and to his surprise HQ had said that this was common among the men at the base too and the allocations of each company were such as to try and send people close to where their own families lived and evacuate them to safe zones that were manned on the perimeter by more soldiers. It wasn't as "safe" as all that, because there were so many gaps in the defences and not enough soldiers to plug them, but it did mean the men fought ferociously, since they were protecting their own families. De Dominicis was assured they would give them similar assignments and take care of the wounded.

The night passed without incident in the mountains, although inhuman howling and ululating could be heard throughout the night, alongside almost constant small arms fire lower down in the valleys.

In the morning they set off again and they had reached the base by early afternoon. The wounded were taken to the medical facilities on base and De Dominicis, D'Amaso, and Tiramino were called in for a debriefing, where the newly appointed ranks of D'Amaso and Tiramino were recognised without question or fanfare, as were several other promotions of various soldiers from private to corporal and so on. But after that, the Colonel in charge of the local brigade had told them the other news.

"You have 80 men with you that are combat trained now and have survived some of the hardest battles anyone ever has. We have had a request from the central command in Rimini. It's an important mission, we need men like you three, and like your battalion for it." Colonel Armani was not related to the famous fashion house by the same name, but certainly was smooth in delivering a shit sandwich Army style, thought De Dominicis. *First they give promotions to my guys, then it's right there with "go get killed you fucker," and "thank you for your service."*

"I realise you're tired and had a bad time of it, but this mission is unique. I will not force any man to go on it, it will be volunteer only, but I hope you all say yes," the Colonel was looking at them hopefully, but none of the three men spoke, De Dominicis was about to just say "no," on principle, with a little smile on his face, but Colonel Armani spoke up again before he could do so.

"It's a mission to go and take out the bastards that did all this. That opened the portals three years ago and opened these last ones too. And to destroy CERN, since that is what permits the portals to open apparently."

Fuck! Thought De Dominicis. The idea to go kill those bastards was really tempting. He felt himself wanting to say "*Yes!*" now.

And it pissed him off.

"Where would this be… Sir?" Asked D'Amaso simply.

"Switzerland. Near Davos."

"And how would we get there, Sir?" Tiramino asked.

"Helicopters. We have enough to get about fifty of you to the drop zone, along with refuelling requirements for later extraction. And you would have air cover from Russian units that are en-route from the East."

"And what exactly is the mission sir?" De Dominicis had finally spoken up too.

"You need to get inside the bunkers we have identified, root out the people responsible and bring them to justice."

"Sir… those bunkers in Switzerland are designed to resist nuclear detonations. How do we get inside?" De Dominicis was extremely suspicious concerning anything the Army told him, even when it was just a simple task, and this one was far from simple.

"You would be provided with high explosives as well as oxyacetylene torches, thermite, and welding lances."

The three men sitting in front of the Colonel's desk kept silent.

"You would also get to pick your own equipment, pretty much anything you wanted."

The silence stretched on.

"And… if you succeed, you could… muster out."

The three men all now looked up at the Colonel intently but still remained silent.

"With commendations."

Now the three men looked at each other, meaningful glances between them that gave De Dominicis the lead, without a word having passed between them.

"We'd want to keep any gear we use even after mustering out, plus a generous contribution in silver, gold, and ammunition, and a decent vehicle for each man too."

The Colonel's face visibly changed colour and his jaw stiffened. Tiramino also noticed a vein in the man's temple became more evident before he spoke again.

"That… well… how much silver and how much gold and what kind of vehicles?"

"Enough that we can fortify our family homes with if we survive, and probably vehicles like armoured Humvees," replied De Dominicis calmly, but also with a hint of aggressiveness in his voice.

"Well, that's a lot of Humvees, we don't have that many on hand…"

"No, but you can get them, and we both know even if we succeed, some of us will die, so it will not be fifty of them, will it?" De Dominicis' aggressive tone remained distinctly present, both in tone as well as on his face.

The Colonel looked down at his desk briefly before replying, "I'll see what I can do."

"We'll want it in writing. For each one of the men who actually volunteers. With their name on it. And we'll want to see the actual silver and gold, vehicles, and ammo are real and here before we set off." De Dominicis was getting ready to stand when the Colonel started to speak, irritated and a little outraged now:

"Look here, you can't just…"

De Dominicis cut him off: "No! You listen here, Colonel, me and my men survived shit you can't even imagine, and if, and I say *if* any of those boys are going back to it, you will meet these conditions, because if you do not, you can find yourself someone else to do it, and if you simply order us to do it we will refuse. What are you going to do? Execute all one hundred of us, including the wounded? Good fucking luck, because we'll be shooting back."

De Dominicis was standing now and the Colonel had started to rise as well, he was almost a foot taller than De Dominicis, but the smaller man did not look in any way intimidated.

"Things have changed, in case you hadn't realised it, what with sitting your ass in that comfortable chair for the last few years, but me and these boys have been fighting monsters from another dimension for three years in a row; and yesterday, and the day before, our entire unit was wiped out except for us. And you are still alive because you were not one of the officers that were with us. And you don't really know shit about how to defeat what you're sending us up against. So, spare me your rank, and your authority, or whatever command structure you still think exists, because I don't give a shit about any of it. We are the only ones who might be able to do the impossible job you want us to do and you will pay what we demand if we manage to do it. And those of us who die still get their share. Their families do. That is all. And we want it in writing. Now either get to it, or find someone else, what will it be?"

Tiramino and D'Amaso had remained seated, watching their Captain bark that whole rant out with a posture that made them wonder if he was about to jump on the Colonel's desk and bite him in the face.

The Colonel, to his credit, stared at De Dominicis in the eye for a few seconds, before he lowered his gaze and nodded silently.

De Dominicis turned and started to head out of the Colonel's office, but he spoke without turning back towards the man:

"I'll have a list of the volunteers within the hour for you."

Tiramino and D'Amaso both stood up and saluted softly, with a little smile on their faces before following De Dominicis out.

11

Taro had spent most of the day with Alessandro and his daughters, noting how they had set up the drones and could send him and Douglas regular updates via a local 4G network Douglas had helped set up between the village of Monte Castello, the surrounding areas, and the military base in Rimini. Taro would have the same live feed Douglas and Alessandro did along with a few other men that co-ordinated the village defences.

Douglas had even managed to convince the Rimini base to hand over two more .50 calibre sniper rifles. He had traded the other two gold disks they had found on the giants for them. Apparently, they would also eventually give Taro a new Humvee, but so far it had not materialised yet. Taro was using his rather abused old sports Mercedes, which had been converted to something that looked mostly like something out of Mad Max. It had metal grills over all the windows that had been welded onto a metal frame that had been bolted onto the body of the car. The .50 Cal didn't fit even in the boot, so Taro had opted for just the shotgun, his Colt Dragoon and Marco in the passenger seat with his SFAR rifle. He'd wanted Marco to meet Alessandro's girls, even if they were several years older than him.

Marco had been quiet mostly, listening and occasionally asking a few questions. The girls had shown him how to control one of the drones and Taro noticed the boy immediately took to it very quickly. *All those hours on the iPad playing Roblox when he was younger might have served for something after all*, he thought.

They were heading back home now and Jordan and Tony had also returned to their homes. Dusk was fast approaching and Taro made it a point to try and be in the house before dark.

As they parked the car and got out, Marco spoke up.

"Dad…?"

Taro turned to look at his son. The boy seemed concerned, but in that calm way of his.

"Yes, son?"

"I think something bad is coming."

The little hair on the back of Taro's neck suddenly stood on end. He had no idea why, but he nodded to Marco.

"Let's get inside quickly."

And they did.

After checking all the doors and windows were secure and all the various precautions of crucifixes, holy water filled pistols, loaded weapons, and garlic too (though no one knew if garlic had any actual effect on Vampires, to date) the Valenti family had sat at the table to have dinner.

They had just finished eating and Taro was uncharacteristically having a coffee, when he asked Marco, "Still have that bad feeling?"

Marco looked at his father, was silent a while, then said:

"I don't know. I think so, but we are safe here now, so maybe it doesn't feel so bad now."

Taro nodded. He knew what his son meant. The men on his side of the family had a hint of that ability that had since been validated even by science years ago. Mostly by a metastudy done by Honorton and Ferrari on precognition. He too had had a kind of sense of things that might come, but since the first werewolf, his own perception of it seemed to be in constant high alert. He couldn't know when he was just being paranoid instead of sensing something. But Marco being a child may have adapted better.

Just as he set his cup down, a sudden very powerful bang and crash happened just outside their front door. Something had either rammed the outer metal cage in front of the door or possibly wrecked it already.

Taro sprang out of his chair, knocking it over, and reaching for the shotgun by the door. It was loaded with alternating silver slugs with holy water pockets in them and silver buckshot also with holy water bubbles in the middle.

The girls had all screamed, except for Alina. She just sat still at the table.

Jane had also sprung up to reach for her own shotgun and Marco now ran past his father to collect his rifle which was leaning against the wall near the door.

The area they were in had a long table in it, the front entrance, a side entrance to the kitchen area, and three windows, a small one near the sink, and two larger ones, one on each end of the long room that comprised the kitchen and eating area in an open plan layout.

Both windows exploded inwards, and long, pale, clawed arms reached in and started to rattle the metal bars that held the creatures outside. The little window exploded inward too though only the fingers of a clawed hand could be seen there. And now the metal cage near the other entrance seemed to receive a shock that could be felt throughout the walls of the house. Taro quickly moved to directly in front of one of the windows, and just as he saw a vampire pull on the metal bars there and start to bend them, he fired a full load of buckshot in its face. He managed to catch a glimpse of the thing's head catching fire and making that howling hiss that denoted their imminent dissolution to burning ash.

One down, fuckers. He thought. Marco had screamed too and jumped back, away from the other window, even if he had not been within grasp of it. He shouldered his rifle though and fired at the arm he could see poking into the room from it. The reports within the confines of the large room were deafening. Jane was shouting at the girls to all get upstairs while she guarded the approach to the stairs. Taro went closer to the window he had just killed one of the vampires from to see if he could see anything outside, even if he remained out of range of any arms that could come through it. He pushed the flashlight button on the shotgun and shone the light out through the window. He saw a fleeting shadow move back too quick to fire at, and another further away, near Jane's car, close to where the forest near their home started.

"Marco, keep away from the windows, and if anything pokes in from that window you shoot it, just like you have been doing, ok?"

"Yes dad." The boy had not turned to look at his father, his eyes were set on the window, his rifle shouldered.

"Good boy, and don't be scared, we have rifles, they need to be scared of us, alright? Keep calm inside and shoot anything that moves near that window."

"Okay."

Taro now moved to the front door to peep through the spy hole. There were two vampires pulling at the bars of the outside cage, and it was bending. In a few more seconds they could make a gap large enough to get through. He took a calculated risk and popped the inner door open quickly, then fired the shotgun directly at the two fiends, but he had a slug in now, and though it seemed to hit the body of one, as a flaming light flashed directly behind it, they both moved away so fast, he couldn't be sure, and didn't get a chance to fire again at them. He left the inner door open though, shotgun shouldered, ready to fire again, and this round would be buckshot. But they were not coming near this door. Instead he heard another loud thud on the cage at the other door. *They were trying to get in there now!*

"Marco, you cover that window. Jane, stand here, in front of the door, blast anything that comes up to it, I need to check the other door!" He moved quickly to the door near the kitchen sink but he didn't bother to check the spy hole this time, he slammed open the gun port, stuck the shotgun barrel in it and pulled the trigger.

The shriek and sudden flash of light that came through the port-hole told him he had got at least one more. He put his eye to the spy hole then, but there was just a burning cloth falling to the ground already. There was at least one more of the things out there. And probably more. He had never even heard of a concentrated attack by multiple vampires. *This is bad. Very bad.*

"Do not open that door Taro! And close this one too!" Jane was standing in front of the main entrance, shotgun at the ready, but she was afraid something else could fly in through those bars and into their home.

Taro came over and closed the door again.

"Marco, you see anything?"

"No dad. And I don't think I hit the thing's arm when I shot. I was kind of scared."

"That's okay boy, you did perfect. You fired and did everything right."

"But I missed."

"Sometimes that happens. But the important thing is you didn't freeze. You acted. You fired and scared the vampire off."

The girls were all huddled on the staircase leading to the upstairs bedrooms. Anna had Alina on her hip, she'd picked her up, and Arianna was huddling with Scarlet.

"Girls, make sure you have your crucifixes in hand, get them from your room and the holy water pistols too, okay? Get them now."

The girls started to get to their room hesitantly, and it was then that Taro thought of it: Vampires can jump and move so fast and high… the upper room window bars were not as sturdy as the downstairs ones… He started to run up the stairs, almost knocking Jane over to get past.

He was nearly at the top of the stairs when he saw Anna was reaching for the light switch in their room.

"Stop, get down!" He screamed loudly. "Down, Down!"

Anna had switched the light on, just as he had started speaking, and then Taro went into that extreme mode where time seemed to slow down. He saw the window opposite Anna burst inwards, the blue curtain enveloping the creature entering through that smaller window, he could not shoot as Anna was still reacting, slowly, ever so slowly, dodging, dropping, half-covering her face with her left arm, the right arm only half-holding Alina as they were falling down towards the floor. He had buckshot, he was pointing the shotgun barrel just above Anna's head, Alina was looking at the blue-shrouded monster that was heading towards them…

Taro pushed off his leg, stepping over the last two steps in a leap…

The creature had landed in the room. Anna was frozen half-crouched, Alina had landed on her feet and was looking towards the monster hooded in the blue curtain…

Taro was not going to make it.

He reached forward with his left hand, holding the shotgun only in the right, trying to pull Anna out of the way, just as the Vampire ripped the curtain that had been covering it off its face, the terrible maw of its open mouth filled with those sharp teeth stretching open, Anna's head still in the way, Alina standing facing the monster, her right little hand going up, towards the creature, probably to ward it off. *They were so fast, so fucking fast, he was still too far please God, no…*

The creature seemed to stop, hesitate, look, directly at Alina, hiss at her, and now Taro's left hand had reached Anna's head, shoving it out of the way to his left just enough for the shotgun barrel to move past her and, one-handed, pointing it directly at the obscenity standing in his children's room, just as the creature switched its attention from Alina to Taro, Taro pulled the trigger.

Jane had been running behind Taro, but was too far to be of use, she saw and heard the shot Taro had fired, but her brain did not understand what it was seeing because it looked as if Taro's shotgun had exploded and a fireball had gone off in the kids' room, which she saw Taro kick away from him and the kids.

The vampire had moved towards Taro just as he had pulled the trigger, and the speed of the creature was such that it had placed its head directly in front of the shotgun's bore. The buckshot cloud was so concentrated it burst the vampire's head into flame instantly and the rest of the thing's body followed suit. Taro had instinctively shot out a front kick at the flaming body and it had landed on Alina's lower bunk bed, a couple of meters away, burning the sheets there.

Taro didn't bother with that and instead pumped the shotgun, and instantly fired a shell directly out of the window, even though nothing had seemed to be there. He wasn't taking chances. He loaded another buckshot round in and kept it pointed at the burst window. Herding the kids back out of the room. The smouldering of Alina's bed was dying down. He pulled the door closed and held it.

"Jane, keep your shotgun trained on the windows in our bedroom. If anything moves there, shoot."

Jane just nodded and went into their bedroom shotgun shouldered, but there was nothing amiss there.

Taro called Marco up too, who came up the stairs backwards, keeping his rifle pointed at the window he had been guarding.

He got everyone into the master bedroom and locked the solid door there, before sitting next to Jane, each of them pointing their shotgun at one of the two windows there.

"The fucking things are trying to get in the house. They may well manage it now. That window in their bedroom is fucked." More than speaking to Jane he was thinking out loud.

"I still don't get why it hesitated, but thank God it did."

"I stopped it daddy. Vampires are scared of God. You told me."
It was Alina speaking to her father, He turned to look at the little
blonde girl with her penetrating blue eyes and her little fist
clutching her tiny silver crucifix, which she wore around her
neck, as did all of them.

Taro was stunned. He looked at the small crucifix, then Alina's
eyes, and then at the small cross again.

"You... you had that in your hand? You pointed it at the
vampire?"

Alina nodded.

It made sense. He had seen her raising her arm at it... he thought
she was just trying to ward off the inevitable...

"Oh God... Thank you!"

He hugged her, but only with his left arm, pulling her close and
kissing her head and saying "thank you, thank you," and "good
girl, you're so smart," and the whole time he kept his shotgun
pointed at the window and one eye on it even as he praised her.
She had probably saved them all.

There was another thud at the cage outside the kitchen door.

Taro let go of Alina and spoke up now.

"Anna, get on the radio, there, on my bedside table. Call Douglas
and tell him we are being attacked by a co-ordinated group of
vampires, so to be on the lookout, and to call Alessandro and send
his drones out here so we know what is going on." Then he turned
to Marco.

"Marco, come here. You sit here, lean your rifle on the bed, here,
put a pillow under it, ok, good, it's pointing at that window, yes,
do not look away from there, no matter what goes on behind here,
ok? I might need to shoot, or your sisters might scream, you
ignore it all and if that curtain twitches even just a little bit, you
shoot, and you keep shooting out that window. Okay?"

Marco nodded. And Taro knew the boy would do as he was told. He had that hunter's instinct to know when to wait and be patient and not get distracted.

Anna was on the radio and Douglas had already replied they had put their own home and the village on high alert and contacted Alessandro to send one of the drones over the Valenti property.

The crash from below happened again, but Taro heard a much softer noise that really got him worried. The door to the kids room had creaked open. Another one, or God knows how many, had got in and was just outside their locked bedroom door.

"Anna, Scarlet, Arianna, spray the floor in front of the door with holy water, now! Make it all wet. The door too. Alina, darling, you stand behind mommy with your crucifix in your hand pointing at the door and if one of those things come in you say…?"

"Vade Retro Satanas," Replied Alina. She pronounced the R a little more like an L, but it would do. It was the intent that counted after all.

"Perfect. Good girl." And as he said it, he pointed his shotgun at the door.

There was another crash and the sound of twisted metal at the kitchen door below them.

Then the bedroom door exploded inwards and Taro fired, as did Jane. The vampire that had crashed through had a lot of momentum but the double buckshot load saw to it that it caught fire, shrieked, shrivelled and burnt just inside the broken splinters of the door.

"Keep your eyes on the window Marco," said Taro, without turning to look at his son.

"I am dad."

"Good boy," he said as he racked a solid slug into the shotgun. There were loud thumps from below but they stopped after the third bump. They had not broken in either.

The only opening was that window in the kids room, but it was enough. Now he and Jane faced the broken door. And Taro had no idea how many of these vampires were out there. They had already killed at least three, probably four, and there was more of them out there.

Time seemed to stand still, then the radio crackled and Elena's voice could be heard coming through it:

"Hi, Elena here. You seem to have two undead near your home and a human just off the side, inside the treeline. Over."

Taro glanced quickly at Anna, who responded:

"Where are the undead? Over."

"They are going round the side of the house. They seem to be… they just jumped up on the lower roof…"

They are going to come in from the kid's window again! Taro thought of rushing out there and getting ready to shoot as soon as they tried to go through the window, but he hesitated. Maybe others had already got in the house and were waiting to ambush him if he stepped out. He could see the door to the children's room from here, he angled himself better and aimed at it, but quickly racked the shotgun again, putting a buckshot shell in place of the slug he had. The radio continued transmitting Elena's voice:

"They are… Oh my God they got into your house I think from a window, I can't see them anym…"

Taro fired. He had seen a shadow flicker towards the door of the children's room, and he knew how fast these things were. He had hit something, because a shrieking flame in human form ran past in front of their broken door and towards the railing at the top of the stairs. And judging from the play of light, it had gone over that railing and landed in the kitchen. Or maybe its ashes had.

Quickly reloading he waited to see if he could see the other one.

Anna spoke into the radio:

"Elena, my dad just shot one of those two. Can you see the other one? Over."

"No, it's inside your house somewhere. Outside I can only see one human, at least the heat signature is that of a human. He is standing on the edge of the forest outside your front door. Over."

Who the fuck is standing outside with at least six vampires out there? Thought Taro.

"Ask her if there is anything else outside other than that guy."

Anna did as Taro had asked, but the reply from Elena was the same. Just that lone human. And a couple of squirrels in the trees. No other animals even.

Fuck it. Thought Taro. He called Anna over and traded places with her, handing her his shotgun, then he reached up in the little alcove above the Imperial sized matrimonial bed and grabbed the large silver crucifix there. He took the Colt 1911 out of the bedside drawer where he kept it, checked it was loaded with the silver and holy water solids, and headed for the broken door. Internally he had filled himself with an absolute level of faith he did have but rarely relied on.

"No, Taro, don't!" Jane had understood what he wanted to do and she was terrified.

"I'm fine. I got God on my side, and a Colt .45." He smiled to himself but in truth he wasn't scared. Alina had made a vampire hesitate and she was just five years old. The pure innocence and faith of a child had made the thing hesitate just long enough, and that's all Taro needed.

"Jesus, Taro, *please!*" Jane's voice was about to stray into the hysterical.

Taro's reply was firm. Harsh even. There was no doubt in it.

"Jesus is right. Now be still woman. And if anything comes through that door too fast you shoot, and don't never mind if I am in the way or not. You shoot. You too Anna." He had not turned back towards them. He was leaning down and sideways to fit through the broken pieces of door that still hung to the hinges.

He had not seen anything flit past from the kids room, so it was probably still in there. Though he couldn't see the whole room, especially the part of it that bent at ninety degrees where Anna slept. At least the light was still on in there. He quickly glanced to the right and the stairs, but saw nothing there.

"Ok, I am going after it. Anything goes in front of this door that is not me after I tell you I am coming back, you both shoot, you got it?"

A subdued but loud enough "Yes" came from both Jane and Anna.

Taro steeled himself, crucifix in the left hand, Colt .45 in the right, and a glowing heart filled with God, *Hail Mary Full of Grace! Hail Mary Full of Grace! Ok, here goes. Lord, let me send this fucking thing back to Hell, please. Amen.*

He walked into the children's room as he shouted, "Vade Retro Satanas!"

As soon as he stepped in the doorway, the last vampire rushed at him from the darkened area of the room, around the corner where Anna had her bed. He barely saw the movement, but he had his Crucifix out in front of him and he pivoted while firing and the thing had stopped just short of him, about a metre away hissing. It slashed at him with its taloned hand. At the same time Taro's left arm pulled back fast, almost as quick as the creature's slash, and it narrowly missed his arm, but caught the crucifix so hard it was snapped out of Taro's hand and flung across the room towards Alina's still smouldering bed. The first shot from the Colt in Taro's hand fired just as the crucifix was being touched by the vampire, and hit it high in the stomach. The second shot hit it in the chest and the crucifix had smashed against the bed-post but not yet hit the floor. The third shot hit the thing in the throat and Taro saw the fire out of the back of its neck. Then time seemed to stand still again. The thing had almost glanced towards the Crucifix and was turning back towards him. The fourth shot hit it in the mouth, Taro saw at least three teeth snap off as another jet of flame sprouted out the back of its head. He stepped back, but so very slowly, and the thing was still falling towards him. He was also pushing backwards, it was going to fall on him. The last shot he fired the muzzle of the handgun was nearly touching the thing's brow, and the flame out the back of its bald head was a fountain that joined with the flame coming out the lower wound that had gone through its mouth. As he fell backward Taro also twisted and pushed at the thing's body with his left hand. Its mouth turned towards him, reaching for his face and neck, but missed by a couple of inches, being stopped by the muzzle of the pistol, and Taro's continued twisting and pushing with the pistol and his left hand. He hit the back of his head and part of his right shoulder on the wall behind him, and the lower half of the vampire fell on his stomach and legs, but the thing's head hit the wooden floor boards right next to the gun, and he fired it again directly in its cheek. The thing's head burst into flame and the rest of the body started to as well, as Taro scrambled out from under it shoving it and kicking it away from him and towards the bathroom that was next to the entrance to the children's room.

He quickly stood up, and remembered his instructions to Anna and Jane. He was definitely in their line of sight.

"Don't shoot. It's fine, I am fine!"

They should have shot me already. Fucking women. They never listen. Thank God.

"It's fine, it's dead."

He walked back in and reached for the radio as he popped the magazine out of the Colt and reached for the other loaded one in the drawer with the same hand he had the Colt in.

"Elena, that human still out there by the forest? Over."

"Yes, he's starting to walk downhill though. Over."

"Ok, you keep him in view and tell me where he is going. Don't stop telling me. Over." He clipped the walkie-talkie to his belt, loaded the colt and ran out again.

"Stay here," he shouted behind him.

"Taro!" Jane was exasperated. She knew he was going after that possibly human, possibly super-vampire or whatever the fuck it was out there, and only with his Colt and eight rounds in the gun. *Fucking stupid men! Always thinking either with their dick or in this case with their balls!* She was very angry with him. *God please keep that big stupid… and ok, brave, bastard alive, please. Please. Sorry for swearing! Thank you. Amen. Oh Fuck.*

Taro had opened the front door, closed it behind him, had a couple of seconds of delay trying to open the warped outer door until he kicked it hard after unlocking it when it eventually banged open, and then he was running down the hill at full tilt. There was a moon out, so he could see a bit in the darkness. Elena's voice kept coming on the radio.

"He's in the forest to your left. I assume that's you running down the hill. You are catching up to him. He's going to the right now, he should pop out of the forest just in front of you."

And so he did. He saw a tall man, thinner than Taro though, running downhill in an ungainly fashion. Taro knew the hillside but boar would still dig it up regularly and it was easy to lose your footing, but he was running as fast as he could in big leaps, each step more of a moon-walk sized jump given the slope of the ground. The man in front of him had shaggy hair, it looked like a dirty kind of blonde, and as the man turned to look at Taro chasing him, he saw that the man also had a similarly shaggy beard.

He doesn't look supernatural, thought Taro, with a sense of welcoming impending violence. He didn't want to shoot this guy.

The man in front of him made a noise, maybe a scared "No!" or a yelp, Taro wasn't paying attention to that. He had seen the man's eyes. And he saw fear.

Good. You should be afraid. And you will be very afraid when I catch you. Taro was gaining on him, he was now only a couple of meters away from the man, who turned and tried to accelerate, but it was too late, Taro was on him. The man tried to change direction to the left, back towards the forest, but Taro leapt to the side too and rammed him with his left shoulder, holding the Colt out to the side with his finger in the trigger guard but away from the trigger, and his thumb holding the hammer back. The man went tumbling and rolling and Taro stumbled but remained on his feet, taking a few awkward steps, running next to the rolling man. As soon as the man came to a stop, belly up, Taro pointed the Colt at him and fired a round into the man's knee area. The man screamed in panic more than pain thought Taro.

Davide reached for his knee but didn't drop the small black orb he held. Taro saw it.

"Drop that black orb or the next shot is in your dick."

"No, don't. The vampires will kill us if I drop it."

Taro noticed that he had hit the man above the knee. Probably had not hit the bone. Mostly a flesh wound. *Lucky. Lucky, lucky.* He thought as he slowly dropped the hammer on the Colt.

He dropped to his own knees next to the man as he brought the butt of the pistol down hard into the man's face. Twice. Blood splattered Taro's face on the second strike. The man was trying to fend him off, but Taro was larger and caught the man's right wrist with his left hand and struck the man's face three more times. Hard enough to cut and hurt, not hard enough to crack the skull or kill him. As the man tried to hide his face he'd naturally rolled over and Taro slid downhill with him, grabbed a handful of the shaggy hair and pushed the man's face into the dirt while shoving the muzzle of the Colt in the back of the man's head.

"You are either going to do exactly what I tell you or I will shoot you in the head right now and I will take that fucking black ball from you."

"Okhai, Okhai!" Came the muffled response.

"Put that thing in your pocket and then raise your hands above your head."

Davide did as he was told, and Taro walked him back up the hill, keeping the Colt pressed against the part of the skull just above the spine and with a death grip on the man's hair, keeping his blood-soaked face turned slightly up towards the moon.

A few minutes later he had Davide securely tied, zip-tied, and taped to a metal chair he had got Jane to bring in from the patio.

The children had all seen him do it and Scarlet asked:

"Will I need to feed this guy like I did Douglas?"

"No darling. We ain't feeding this guy. In fact, you get back in our bedroom with mommy and everyone else and stay there. Don't peek and don't come out until I say."

Jane was looking at him and shaking her head, silently asking him not to do this. He looked at her coldly. She knew. This guy had been controlling the vampires somehow. She knew Taro knew. And she knew he was right.

"At least let me put some music on."

Taro nodded.

Then he taped Davide's mouth shut before he went to get the pliers, a metal file, a piece of hard rubber tubing that had been left over from some plumbing work, and a lighter with a long beak.

He laid them all out on the table in front of Davide then sat across from him, looked him in the eyes and spoke.

"I am not going to fuck around. In fact, to show you I am not, I am going to rip one of your ears off without even asking you a single fucking thing. Then I'll crunch a finger or two. After that I'll have a little drink, then I will take that tape off your mouth for one minute. If you scream when the tape is off, I'll put it back on and then I will dig your left eye out with a teaspoon. And cut off a few toes. So… I suggest you don't scream when I eventually take the tape off. What I suggest you do instead is talk. At a normal voice, and you will tell me immediately all the important things first. Leaving nothing out. If after one solid minute, that is, exactly sixty seconds you have not told me all the important things first, I will put the tape back on and burn one eye out and rip the other ear off. If I feel you didn't share the most important things and held back a little, I'll do the same. In fact, if I am not really happy that I understand *exactly* what happened here tonight, and why, and who made it happen, I will do the same anyway. So, I suggest you speak well and quickly. Now concentrate, because this will hurt, but then you will know that, like I said, I am not fucking around."

Then Taro took the pliers, pinched Davide's left ear with them, and holding the man's hair in his left fist ripped off a strip of ear. Davide was trying to scream through the tape but making gurgly noises mostly, as his broken nose was not letting him breathe too well. Then Taro took the man's little finger in the pliers and crushed the second joint of it and twisted it until it broke. The gurgly noise was louder then fainter, and there was a lot of blood spraying from the man's broken nose. He crunched the ring finger next. The screaming was more subdued. He came round the front, held the man's head up by the hair and looked into Davide's eyes.

They were a pale blue he noted, and the man did have a dirty blonde beard and hair. The man's eyes were watering, rolling half-way back, avoiding Taro's own eyes and the broken nose was barely letting enough air in to keep him conscious.

Good. He thought. He took out his knife and poked a hole in the tape where he figured the lips came together. Davide jerked back. He'd hit some teeth, maybe a lip. *Oh well. A bit more air going in though.* Then he went to the fridge and pulled out a corona. Took his time cutting a slice of lime and putting it in the bottle. Then went back to his chair, took a sip. Got up again, took the kitchen timer his wife used sometimes and put one minute on it.

Looking at Davide he waited a little. The man was looking back at him now. Taro took another sip of the beer.

"Ready? After I take the tape off you have one minute. I suggest you start with your name and surname and then rattle off all the things that matter. Quickly. Remember what happens next if I am not happy I understood exactly what happened here tonight, why and by whose orders."

The man nodded emphatically.

Taro took the tape off and even before he could start the timer the man had started speaking quickly in Italian.

"Davide Soffiaforte. I am the number three freemason in Emilia Romagna. My boss is Samuele Schwartz. He ordered me to come here with six shades and take out your family. Another man, Andrea Cuccala, has another six shades and will try to kill Douglas Jones. Neither of us was told why exactly we had to kill you and your family, other than you are preventing the plans of the Princes from going to fruition. I don't know the names of the Princes. Only Samuele Schwartz may know the names, maybe not even him, or maybe only one or two of the names. There are six princes, one for each continent. Except Antarctica, that is ruled by the Watchers. Planar beings from another dimension. I don't know much about them. They may be the Nephilim of the

Bible, I don't know. The black orb in my pocket is how I controlled the shades, they follow my commands as I think of them, but only those six and only after a ritual was done to pass control to me. I don't know where the black orbs come from. I don't know how Samuele Schwartz got the black orbs or how he learnt to control the shades. I can give you the address of the freemason Temple where he resides in San Marino. It's...."

Taro held up a finger.

"Your minute is up, but so far you did well. Now shut up."

He put the tape back over the man's mouth. Then got on the radio.

"Douglas, come in, over."

"Here, over."

"I got a guy here, he was controlling six vampires, they managed to break into our house and I managed to get them all luckily, but there is another guy coming to you with also six vampires, they are normal humans but they control the vampires telepathically through some kind of big black marble the have. I know your place is more secure than mine, but don't go outside. Over."

"Got it. Thanks. I'll ask Elena to keep the drone up over our place. I was listening in. Thanks. Over."

"No problem. Be careful, and let us know when you spot them. Over."

"Will do. Over."

"Right. Now where were we? Ah yes, you're going to tell me a whole bunch more things. Names, addresses, all sorts. Leave nothing out. Because I can sense things. Like when you said you were to kill us. That wasn't the whole story, now was it. You will tell me next, exactly what the plan was for myself and my children. Let me explain something. I know it was something fully evil and disgusting, but if I sense you didn't tell me the whole story, I will skin you alive and feed you to yourself piece by piece. Got it?"

114

The man nodded quickly.

It was going to be a long, unpleasant night, thought Taro.

And it was; but he did get all the information he wanted.

12

Douglas was in his watchtower, his .338 Lapua resting easily on its bipod. Elena had told him she had seen a human with six shades approaching his property 15 minutes ago. Now he could see the man through the scope. A rather squat, wide man with a bit of a salt and pepper beard. He had six vampires walking next to him, arranged in a circle around him.

Eight hundred meters. He compensated for the man's walk. Held his breath. Squeezed the trigger. The report was loud but Douglas had his ear protection on. The man dropped like a rag doll and not even a second later the vampires were on the body, biting chunks out of it. Douglas fired again, and then again, he had destroyed two of the vampires before the others scattered. One had jumped several metres up a tree and was scanning the general area. Douglas shot it and it caught fire and fell to the bottom of the evergreen tree. Luckily the fire was localised and died down quickly, without setting the forest alight.

He could not see the other three, they had scattered fast, but Elena had kept observing and was still tracking two of them, they were running fast, away from him. She directed him but for a while he could not see any of them despite the excellent night-vision scope he had on the rifle. Slowly, with some direction he found one of them standing near a tree. Elena had the drone hovering high up above it and Douglas could see the creature was looking straight up. They must have sensitive hearing of some kind, because Douglas was sure it was trying to see the drone.

A thousand one hundred and fifty metres. It was far. If the creature held still long enough though… Douglas did a hold with the dots on his fourth generation, long distance military scope. Then gingerly touched the trigger softly, softly, until the kick of the rifle surprised him. He quickly adjusted the scope again and he could see the huge flare in the night scope even at this distance. When they went up in flames, they really were easy to see at night. Elena tracked one of the remaining two vampires until it went too far for her to risk the drone and she brought it back. There were still two of the things out there, but he certainly had an easier time of it than what the Valenti had from the little he had heard from Taro. *But he's caught the human that had been controlling them alive.* How the hell he had done that Douglas had no idea. It was as if Taro just had a natural talent for killing. *And hunting, too apparently.* But he certainly excelled at killing things. *The way that man's brain works,* thought Douglas, not wanting to imagine what it must be like to have that constant underlying level of... *what was it even? Paranoia? Killer instinct? Just sheer brutal innate deadliness? Were normal people even born that way, or did he become like that?* Douglas thought about asking the man one day.

Either way, glad he's on our side. If he can take out six vampires from a co-ordinated surprise attack, he might be deadlier than the things coming out of the portals. He prepared to clean and put away the Lapua, and then he wanted to go over to the Valenti at first light. He would tell Taro over the radio.

13

It was barely dawn when Douglas pulled up outside the Valenti's place and he immediately saw the outside cage to the main entrance was badly warped and didn't close properly. He had had Elena keep a scan active so he knew the area was clean, but he still felt tense and had his hand on his holstered Colt 1911 as he went to knock.

The door opened after a few seconds, Taro let him in and Douglas was surprised to see the whole family sitting at the usual table, having a very early breakfast. The kids still in their pyjamas and looking sleepy and their hair uncombed. Jane too looked a little worn. Her hair was in a rough bun and she had a t-shirt and tracksuit pants on. She greeted Douglas but he could see her mind was elsewhere. She was worried. He made a point to remind himself to send some people over to rebuild the cages.

As Taro offered him coffee, he told Douglas what had happened. Douglas mentioned redoing all the window-bars in a much more reinforced fashion, and he saw Jane visibly release some tension when he said it. The internal doors too. In fact, Douglas invited the whole family to stay at his place until the works were complete. Jane thanked him profusely. The poor woman was stressed out of her mind. Taro and the kids seemed fine though.

And Arianna, who had uncharacteristically kept quiet while Taro talked, now that she had finished her eggs, spoke up.

"Daddy tied a man to a chair, like he did with you when he met you. But this one is not going to become our friend." She shook her head seriously.

"No," said Scarlet, "Dad wouldn't even let us feed him, poor man," she made a sad face, but also shot a quick glance at her father, who seemed about ready to spit some venom directly out of his eyes at her. She quickly added, while watching her dad, "But after all, he did try to get vampires to kill us, so he's not a nice man like you. And he probably doesn't even like porridge, like you!" She made an airplane noise with her spoon, which she then wisely shoved in her own mouth while looking at Douglas now, reminding him of the humiliation she had subjected him to when Taro had first let Douglas in when all the creatures had started appearing.

Douglas, a little disconcerted by Taro's daughters, looked at Taro with a question in his eyes, "Where is he?"

"In the downstairs bathroom. He's not going anywhere. And I have a bunch of names and addresses and notes here. See if you want to ask him anything else and we can go and get it out of him."

Douglas took the notebook and started to read, paging through the ten pages of notes in it that Taro had made. There was a little spatter of what might have been blood droplets on one page and some kind of greasy smudge on another page. He dreaded to think what the guy in the downstairs bathroom looked like and was glad he had not been here for the questioning. When he finished reading everything, he looked at Taro and said:

"I can't think of anything. Seems you got it all."

Taro just nodded, drank the last of his coffee and said, "I need some help to get him in your Humvee and we can get him to the base for any further questioning as soon as the reinforcements arrive to take my family to your place."

"Sure."

"Ok kids, finish up and get upstairs with Mom and get dressed. You guys will go to Doug's house and me and Douglas are gonna take that bad guy off to prison."

A few minutes later, two Humvees had taken Jane and the Valenti children away to Douglas' home.

Taro and Douglas had removed Davide from the chair he had been tightly strapped into, though he was still trussed up with his arms tied behind his back.

The left ear was now just a ragged hole with coagulated blood all down the man's shirt, four of his fingers were horribly twisted, the skin on them broken and they were purple and black, the zip ties so tight the man's hands were swollen, and part of his beard had been burnt off and his skin was bubbling on the left cheek where clearly open flame had been applied. The man's nose and lips were cut and broken and he looked barely conscious. He made moaning noises through the duct tape over his mouth as they walked him up the stairs, and outside into the back of the Humvee; each man holding him up by his upper arm on each side.

Once they were in, Taro sat next to Davide, and Douglas started driving towards Rimini. When they were about a third of the way there, on one of the country roads Taro asked Douglas to stop the Humvee.

"Why?" asked Douglas suspicious. It was a bright, sunny day, but he had a bad feeling about this.

"I need a piss, so does he," said Taro casually, "he's been tied to that chair all night. Unless you want the smell of piss in your Humvee?"

Douglas said nothing but pulled over. Taro got up, and opened the back door. Then, as Douglas turned in his seat to say he'd come help. He saw Taro grab the man by the hair hard and bodily shove him out of the door with such force that the man could not help but fall out of the door badly, landing on the hard asphalt outside with a sickening crunch. Taro was out of the Humvee before Douglas could rush out his door and run around. When he did, he saw Taro had his Colt out in his hand and was kicking the man towards the deep ditch by the side of the road.

"No, Taro, wait! Stop!" Douglas reached out towards Taro quickly walking next to him, but some instinct of self-preservation made him not touch Taro.

Taro had kicked the man into the ditch, who was now lying prone, face up at the sky, his swollen eyes half-conscious yet panicked, tired beyond any human Douglas had ever seen. And Taro jumped in the ditch with the man, one leg on either side of him, the Colt pointed at the man's face.

"No Taro don't, we still can get more out of him!"

Taro ignored Douglas completely, as if the man's words had not even reached him or as if Douglas wasn't even there.

"Rot in Hell, you piece of shit," said Taro calmly, looking directly in Davide's eyes, before the too loud and too inhuman report of Taro's Colt made Douglas jerk and stand still.

Taro just stood there for a second, looking at the now dead man with a .45 calibre sized hole in his forehead. The blood draining out of the back of the man's shattered skull was seeping through the grass and soil beneath and could not be seen yet, so the hole looked unnaturally neat even if the eyes were slightly more opened now, the overpressure in the cranium giving Davide more of an awake look in death than he had in the last seconds of his life.

Everything was still for a few seconds, then Taro turned to look at Douglas and Douglas saw something he had not seen before in Taro. It took him the rest of the drive back in silence for him to put some words to it. The man had looked a strange mix of tired, or sad, or melancholy to a degree that was almost palpable in the electrified air between them. *Hurt,* thought Douglas later. *A hurt he didn't let anyone ever see,* he figured, and yet, underneath it all, even deeper there was a fire, an intensity in the man that reminded Douglas of a forest fire he had seen once, from a distance, when he had lived in America. He had thought it was some vision of Hell. A force of nature so hot and implacable human beings seemed weak and irrelevant before it. It had burnt for days even with helicopters dumping water on it. Taro had a microcosm of that somewhere behind his sadness, tiredness, and hurt. A compressed fire of rage or maybe just intensity, that could not be put out. Like the centre of a tiny but eternal red sun; and with that look in his eyes, Taro had spoken:

"You didn't hear for the whole night what he had planned for my wife, and worse, for my children. I made him me tell me. All of it. And there was nothing more to get out of him Doug. I got it all. May that piece of shit rot in the lowest pit of Hell for all eternity. I understand why Hell exists now, and it's for things like him."

After that Douglas didn't say anything. They just got back in the Humvee and drove back to Taro's place in silence.

14

Back at the Valenti's place, Douglas and Taro sat at the main dining table, a kitchen towel bunched up under it, they were staring at the fist-sized black orb Taro had taken from the now defunct Davide. He had used folded over disposable kitchen towels to take it from the sink in the bathroom where he had kept it along with trussed up Davide earlier.

Taro had told Douglas that if he touched it with bare skin he got flashes of absolutely demonically evil shit that he did not want to experience again. Douglas reminded them both of a similar experience he had had before he'd met Taro, when the squad he had been with had been wiped out by werewolves. They had found a kind of black stone that Douglas had touched and it is where the image of what Cooper had labelled as the Gibbering Mouther had flashed into Douglas' mind.

Now, the scientist in him made him reach out with a tentative left index finger. They had to test it. Taro refused to do it anymore, saying he had touched it several times when he had taken it off Davide, and he was sure the experience was as horrifying each time.

Douglas touched the very tip of his index finger to the black orb and snapped it back instantly, his face had blanched slightly.

"Yup. Demonic shit," he said simply. Taro didn't ask. He didn't want to know and he wished he could forget the things he had seen when he had touched it three times last night. The last time by accident. After a short silence, Douglas spoke again.

"What I don't get is how that guy was holding it and carrying it around. I mean… no one gets used to that kind of imagery. A full minute of it is probably enough to make anyone insane."

"I have a theory," said Taro, "That guy, Soffiaforte, he said they had to do some disgusting rituals before getting the orb. A kind of perverse and inverted version of a... I don't know. Some kind of Black Mass. I think it gives the Satanists the power to hold on to the black orbs and control the... demon-things that come through the portals. That's what he said anyway, that he controlled them with his mind. He just thought of what he wanted them to do and they would do it. Like extensions of his mind."

"Hmmm..." said Douglas pensive. "So, you figure because we are baptised Catholics we get the... full experience instead?"

Taro shrugged. "Makes sense to me. And it sort of works in reverse too, right? If it didn't, I wouldn't have been able to get that last vampire we had in the house. They are kept at bay to some extent, by our faith and silver crosses; and this black orb seems to be their version of our silver crosses. Well, not exactly analogous, but you know what I mean."

"Yes. I need to get this to the lab and study it. Frequency, harmonics, EM fields, the lot. Maybe it can give us some answers or a new way to deal with the things."

"Sure," replied Taro, "but that takes time. Now I want you to take us to Rimini. And convince whoever we need to convince there to give us three helicopter gunships and a few special ops guys. I plan to wipe out every fucking freemason temple, mansion, house and every freemason in them from the face of the Earth."

Douglas started to try to explain that as a general rule, American Generals and military commanders didn't tend to do as host nation civilians wanted, but he remembered the look in Taro's eyes from earlier and decided to himself: *You know, what, let whichever Generalissimo try to tell Taro that himself.*

After checking on the radios that Jane and the children were safely at Douglas' house along with Douglas' wife and children, they were on the way to Rimini within minutes. The black orb safely stored in a cardboard box packed with disposable paper kitchen towels.

General Malcom Terrence Vaude the Third, was a fourth-generation military man with distant French roots that were lost in the mists of the French revolution. He was the current head of the American Rimini Base, though he liaised closely with his Italian counterpart, a Generale Massimo Aviliani. The conference room in which they met Douglas and Taro had both men along with a Major-General Briggs, which Taro had met before, right when all the madness and portals had begun. There was also an Italian equivalent to Major-General Briggs, but Taro had not paid attention when the introductions were made —he had been studying Vaude— and for the life of him he could not recall what the rank or the name of the Italian man were.

After a brief introduction, Douglas explained in rather diplomatic terms what Taro had discovered and how the Freemasonic chapter in Rimini was responsible for the directed assault on both the Valenti and Jones homes. Douglas spoke for a long while, giving plenty of details and handing out copies of the notes Taro had made, which were not always very legible or detailed, so Taro went over them for clarity, limiting himself to reading them out in full. When he had finished he asked if he may express some thoughts. Vaude said, yes along with the others who all nodded.

"So…" started Taro, "this is not going to sound "nice" or polite, but it is factual and important. We need to kill every Freemason that exists and I would like to start right away with the San Marino temple, where the bastard that wanted to have my children raped and tortured as well as eaten alive is still probably hiding and I would like to get him alive and make him tell us more things, which I am sure I can get him to do. I know you all have your procedures, and ranks and military hierarchy, but frankly, gentlemen, all of that is not relevant or important right now. We are fighting an enemy that comes straight out of Hell and doesn't respect any kind of Geneva convention or hierarchy, except maybe whatever version of it Hell has. I want this guy Samuele, and I want him alive. We should be heading there right now. And you're not going to find anyone better than me for motivation or ability. So, give me a team and as many helicopter gunships as you can spare and I will bring him back here in a couple of hours."

He had got it all out fast and in one breath.

He looked at the men's eyes. *Vaude was a bureaucrat. Goddamit!* he thought.

"Well, while we appreciate all you have done, Mr. Valenti, we cannot simply put a military team under your command, the training alone…" before Vaude could even complete the sentence Taro had pushed his chair back, looked General Aviliani straight in the eyes, the Italian General was older, chances were small, but still, he had to try… and he spoke in Italian:

"General, questo non capisce un cazzo. Lei me li da degli uomini, o devo andare a fare tutto da solo come per gli ultimi tre anni?"

Vaude did not speak Italian well at all, but he understood *cazzo*. The Italian for *dick,* which was used in that language somewhat analogously to the word *fuck* in English.

Douglas had understood perfectly however, and wanted to hide his head in his hands. Taro's concept of diplomacy probably hailed from Sparta. He'd just told the Italian general *"This guy doesn't understand a fucking thing. Will you give me some men or do I need to go and do this by myself like for the last three years?"* which wasn't even fair. The American military had upgrade Taro's home to a veritable fortress, given him plenty of equipment and ammunition and logistic support. Douglas knew what was driving Taro, but this was not the way to approach things. He hung his head trying to think how to contain the damage, but Taro was not waiting.

"No? E allora andatevene a fanculo tutti quanti."

"No? So you can all go fuck yourselves."

Aaaand… exit Taro, thought Douglas.

The rest of the room was still sitting in a slight stunned silence. Douglas lifted his finger and spoke quickly.

"General… Generals, gentlemen… please give me a minute with the man. You must understand, he single-handedly killed six vampires, captured the man that was controlling them, figured out the mechanism of that… and his family is specifically targeted. As is mine, and it was his warning that permitted me to defend mine much easier than he had to deal with it. Please, you must understand… he also made the man that was controlling the vampires explain… in excruciating detail, what they do with children, his children, when… if they get them, in order to… produce the kind of… rituals that permit them to control the Hellspawned." The silence remained, so Douglas continued.

"It is very likely if we do not move very quickly that the head of the Freemason temple in San Marino will go underground and disappear if we don't move fast. That man, Taro Valenti, has single-handedly been the most valuable man we have had since the portals started in terms of understanding how to defeat the things that come through the portals. A few days ago he shot down a red dragon. Gentlemen, please, let me speak with him and get some teams ready. I will talk to him, but he is right. And I apologise for his lack of diplomacy, I assure you he is absolutely capable. He's just not… a… people person?" Douglas' smile was cringy even to himself. He excused himself and left, running as soon as he left the room, or else he would not get to Taro before the man drove off towards San Marino in Douglas' Humvee.

"Hey, Taro. Stop. I got you the teams." It was a lie, but Douglas had understood how Taro's mind worked by now.

Taro turned and looked at Douglas with an intensity that scientists might use when trying to spot a new bug under a microscope slide.

"You got me the helis and special ops teams in the last 30 seconds?" Taro's face was a fascinating display of chiselled doubt mixed with sarcasm.

"Yeah. Pretty much. But, you gotta wait here, ok? Just go sit in the Humvee. I have the keys, and I am not giving them to you, but just wait a minute okay? We still need a few minutes to collect a team together, right? Don't do anything stupid. Those Freemason temples probably have dozens of vampires in them. We need more people."

"How long?"

Douglas hesitated. Calculated. Lied again. Secure and convinced in his lie without any hesitation. He knew it was a lie and he was proud. "Half an hour. Forty-five minutes tops. I want to pick the guys myself."

He's lying. Thought Taro. *Fine. Let's see what he can do.*

"Alright. I'll be in the Humvee. In the back. Gonna lie down. I didn't sleep last night." Taro turned and walked away.

"Great. Good. See you in a bit." Douglas said to Taro's back. He was flabbergasted. *And I think he really is going to lie down. I think he actually is. Well, fuck me. Now to get back to the generals and... make miracles happen. God help me.*

‌ॐ•ॐ

It was indeed thirty minutes later, and Taro had not managed to really sleep. He had barely managed to regulate his tension and anger, make it focused, when he heard a thumping on the side of the Humvee. He opened the back door and climbed out.

He was surprised to see General Aviliani there with the other younger man whose name Taro had missed.

"Allora…Signor Valenti…" started the older man, he probably spoke English quite well, but Taro could tell he was going to stick to Italian when speaking to him and using the polite form of address, even if the tone and face were rather sarcastic and a little amused.

"It seems you are a very good tactician but leave something to be desired as a politician eh?"

Taro nodded knowingly. The old man was going to bust his balls for a bit, and so be it, he kind of deserved it.

"Now look, I get you had a difficult night. I can't even imagine, but… we need the Americans. They have a lot of equipment here and it's helped us a lot. They have been generous with you too. So, telling the commander of the base he's a dickhead who doesn't understand anything is probably not the way to go, eh? What do you say?"

Taro nodded again, silently, then spoke softly: "Yes, you're right." He wanted to add to it, explain how the freemasons were probably already gone because they were taking so long, but he knew that was the general Italian trait; to try to shift any guilt or blame. He hated that aspect of his countrymen.

General Aviliani studied the man in silence for a bit, then spoke again.

"Alright, well, let's see what we can do eh? The Americans are loading up a bunch of special forces guys and two helicopters. Captain Ciasco here is the head of a small unit of the Special Group of the Carabinieri. He only has four men. You wanna go with them? We Italians don't have a helicopter gunship available right now, but we have two Jeeps and men who are baptised and not scared."

"Yes. Thank you general."

"Don't thank me yet. You're probably going to get yourself killed if you don't control that anger, and then your wife and kids will grow up in this hell without a father. How tall are you? One ninety? About a hundred kilos?"

Taro was slightly confused by the seeming non-sequitur, but answered anyway, "Yes."

"Okay, go with the Captain."

Taro started to follow the younger man who had not spoken at all and seemed built out granite covered in flesh. His features were chiselled and he could not have been older than early thirties.

Aviliani called out to Taro as he was already moving off.

"Ah, Valenti?" Taro turned to look at the General.

"No fucking around. You do what the Captain says, *as* he says, *when* he says. You're not the boss. He is. You follow his orders, or so help me God I will keep you in a fucking cage and you'll never see daylight again."

Taro nodded and added: "Yes Sir. Thank you, Sir." Then he turned and followed Captain Ciasco.

General Aviliani looked at the two men walking away and wondered about Valenti. *He's not a young man. Over fifty already. Fit. He had an extensive martial arts background, grew up all over, couple of decades in Africa apparently, where he did some security work.* Those files and data were scant. A lot had been lost along with the four billion souls that had perished in the last few years. *But apparently never any military service.* Yet the man seemed to understand things that Aviliani had seen many soldiers fail to grasp. *Special Ops type. Hard to control, a real pain in the ass sometimes, but invaluable on the field. Hopefully Ciasco will not get pissed off and kill him.*

Taro soon understood why Aviliani had asked his height and weight. Ciasco had led Taro soundlessly into a building and some locker-style change room, where four other men were busy putting on what looked like weird riot-gear Taro had never seen before. It was all-black Kevlar-lined armour that included a silver neck ring-guard to prevent attacks to the throat, along with helmets that incorporated metal, judging by their weight and looked like a modern version of an armoured medieval helmet. The chest of the uniforms had a large red cross on them, crusader style.

Captain Ciasco pointed to a rack where different sized armours were standing. He told Taro to get one in his size and put it on.

The other men were faster and finished before he did, one of them helped him without talking, just showing him how to close the clasps and so on. Then they went down a corridor to an armoury.

Each man picked out his own main weapon, but they all had the same version of a black Beretta 93R. Taro had never seen one in person, but the little forward handle in the folded away position was iconic, and he surreptitiously noted that the pistols did indeed have selector switches, single, three-round burst, or fully automatic. These were late 1970s designs almost as old as Taro himself. He wondered at the fact that these guys all had this style of pistol and two spare extended magazines for them too. They also all had a black handled stiletto style blade, not unlike the Gerber Mark II Taro liked. He noted they had small red crosses etched in the black handles. Two of the guys picked up drum-fed automatic shotguns, and Captain Ciasco shouldered a flamethrower backpack. The flamethrower also had what looked like a 5.56 mm assault rifle below it. It was a weird contraption that did not look light. The other two men had MP5s, with extended magazines and four magazines each in their vests. Taro opted for his Colt Dragoon strapped to his right leg and exchanged his 8 shot Winchester pump action for one of the automatic drum-fed shotguns. He'd never shot one like it, but it was a shotgun, with a very short barrel; not exactly rocket science or for precision work. Taro thought he'd make sure Ciasco knew the point was to take at least the Samuele guy alive; because none of these men looked like they would ask too many questions or even hesitate before painting entire rooms with the insides of whatever creature, human or otherwise, they found opposing them in that Freemasonic Temple.

As they headed out to the Jeeps one of the men tapped Taro on the shoulder. Taro had not even been sure it had happened, because inside the Kevlar lined body armours, which included gloves and left nothing exposed to the elements, it was rather muffled, though the helmets had in-built radios that transmitted among the members of the team faultlessly.

"What's your name?" Asked the much younger man, though no less tall than Taro.

"Taro." Then as his polite nerve-cell caught up with him, he asked, "Yours?"

"Marco. Here." He handed Taro one of the stiletto style bladed weapons. It was inside a sheath that had straps you could locate in various positions on the body-armour depending on what loads you had. Taro had taken hold of the thing by the sheath, still looking at it.

"It used to belong to my brother. I want it back after."

"Sure." Said Taro. Once in the Jeep he had taken the time to place the sheath so it was on the left side of his chest, handle-down. Like the other shotgun wielders, he had one large spare drum clipped to his belt somewhat behind and to the right, and his Colt Dragoon strapped to his right leg, where the other men had the Beretta 93Rs.

He had examined the knife and found it had a black blade too and the motif of the red cross was repeated on the blade near the handle, but etched in silver on the black. The cross on the handle was the bright red of the Carabinieri stripe they still had on their normal uniforms. He placed the knife away and looked at the man that had given it to him and nodded at him.

The ride to San Marino only took a little over half an hour at the speed the drivers were going. When they arrived at the temple it was a large villa that had a well-kept garden all around it. Taro was grateful that while it was close to other buildings and homes, it was at least fully detached.

Captain Ciasco led his men into the pedestrian side gate by having one of the men use a long crowbar to break the lock on it.

Taro liked the man's style. He hadn't even glanced at the intercom. With hand-signals he sent one shotgun wielder and one assault rifle guy round the back. He told Taro "You stay with me. On my left. Don't shoot any of my guys or I'll set you on fire."

Taro nodded but the man had not even glanced at him. He was already moving towards the front door.

The other shotgun wielder pointed at the top hinges on the front door and waited.

One of the men from the back spoke in the radio: "In place,"

Ciasco only said "Breach," and the man with the shotgun fired at each hinge then kicked the door in. Loud reports could be heard at the back of the villa too.

As soon as they were in, Taro thought they were too late. The place was empty, a large black and white tiled floor had a grand double staircase going to the first floor and a similar double marble-floored version going underground. As they stepped forward, two side doors, one on each side of the main entrance they had come in from, burst open and two men with AK-47s started shooting. Taro had begun to turn toward the man on his left and felt something hit his left shoulder and a kind of smack on his helmet. He fired roughly at the man, who kept firing. Taro could see the Ak-47s belching flames as he took better hold of the shotgun and rapidly pressed the trigger several times. The man with the AK-47 in front of him started to kind of fold or appear to begin to fragment. The door behind him was also splintering, and Taro got hit in the back hard, like from a baseball bat in his left kidney and another on his left shoulder. He fired two more rounds at the man that now had a halo of pink mist all around him, the wall and door behind him changing colour as if from a faulty, giant pink spray can. Taro turned his head just in time to see two more men at the top of the stairs, just getting in

133

position with assault rifles. He started to run, trying to get under the staircase, but firing one round at each man as he went. It must have had some effect, because the first man, the one closest to him seemed to fall back, and the other one too, though even as he fired, Taro saw there was parts of the bannister the man was kneeling behind already splintering in the air. Some of the other men must be firing too. He reached the top of one of the stairs going down, and keeping his attention to where they curved and became a dark corner around which anything might lurk, he made sure he was under the top part of the stairs above him, so anyone on the first floor would not be able to see him. Looking around, he saw that Captain Ciasco was next to him, and the other two men were in a similar position but on the other side of the room, which was a mirror of their own situation.

"Four men. Neutralised." It was Ciasco's voice in Taro's helmet.

"Alpha good."

"Beta good."

"Charlie good."

"Delta took a few but good. Only bruises."

Ciasco tapped Taro on the helmet then spoke.

"Check my tanks. Any leaks?"

Taro had a good look, while he worried about people rushing them. There was a long black smear on one of the tanks, one round had skipped along there, but there were no holes.

"No, you're good."

"You?" asked Ciasco.

"I don't know. Got hit by something. Not sure if anything got through the armour. I can't feel anything."

"Where?"

"Head. Left shoulder; front and back, and my left kidney hurts like I got a bad kick to it."

Ciasco spun Taro around and checked Taro's lower back. He pushed and prodded a bit, scratched maybe. Then tapped the upper shoulder and checked Taro's helmet.

"Yeah, you got tapped good on the kidney. Edge of the moulded ceramic. Maybe a cracked rib or two. Here. Souvenir."

He handed Taro a flattened round. Taro couldn't tell, but he assumed it was an Ak-47 round that had flattened itself on the edge of the ceramic plate and then went on to tear enough Kevlar to remain caught in the vest. He opened a cargo pocket on his left leg and dropped the squished round in it. The he looked at Cisco and pointing down the stairs asked: "We going down?"

"Sure. Stay on my left. All good. Going downstairs. Alpha, Beta, secure upper staircase." That was the two guys who had come in from the back. And sure enough, Charlie and Delta met Taro and Ciasco at the landing, a metre or two underground compared to the entrance, where there was only a very solid looking double door. It looked wooden, but that was just the veneer. Internally it was a metal door with multiple internal bolts and the frame would be steel embedded in reinforced concrete too.

"Delta, pack the charge."

"Sir." The man that had also apparently been hit, but seemed none the worse for wear opened a small backpack he had on, took out what looked like an alien-shaped claymore mine, pressed it to the centre of the double doors and when it remained attached to it pressed a central button on it that light up bright red.

"Thirty seconds, go!"

Every one of the four men ran back up the stairs and then stepped away from the opening, standing next to Alpha and Beta who were guarding the bottom of the stairs leading to the first floor.

The explosion was loud but not deafening and Taro realised the helmets must have built-in safety levels for muffling sound.

When they returned down to the landing the door had warped and one side had fallen in, the other remained hanging but badly bent. They could get past now and did so. Lights were off, so each man turned on the flashlight integral to their weapon. There was a corridor, and more stairs heading down which then turned on themselves and led to an underground chamber. It was octagonally shaped and had a door in each of its sides except the one they had entered from.

Behind each door various other rooms existed. Some were offices, one let to some kind of throne room with a small altar, another to a larger room with 13 seats arranged around a sunken arena with an altar in its centre. There seemed to be cameras in the corners of this room and the altar was stained with what might have been old dried blood. Behind this ritual room was a metal door that was also locked but had the key inserted in the lock. Strange noises and shuffling could be heard behind it.

Captain Ciasco ordered the other entrance be barred shut before the inner door was to be opened. Whatever was behind that door, he didn't want it to get out of this building. He then got one of the men to be ready to open it while standing to the side of it and be ready to move away from it quickly since every other member of the team was pointing their weapons at the door. Ciasco stood directly in front of it with his flamethrower lit.

Taro was on his left. And the other men in a wide semi-circle in front of it. As soon as the key turned, the door slammed open so fast that the man who had opened it got a fracture on his wrist as he'd been unable to move his hand back quickly enough.

Ciasco and the men with assault rifles, to their credit, all managed to pull their triggers just as they all got hit by a vampire ramming into them. Which meant that three of the vampires were busy already catching fire and turning to ash even as they tried to bite and slash through the fireproof Kevlar armour the men wore.

Taro had hesitated, the drum-fed shotgun had a short barrel for maximum spread and he didn't want a stray round to hit the man that had turned the key. Had he thought about it rationally, the idea was rather silly, since the armours had stopped almost direct hits from AK-47 round at close range. But a lifetime of gun-safety is not easy to let go of instantly, so he got rammed by a long-limbed humanoid that was all teeth and claws and slashing. The shotgun was useless as it had been pushed down and Taro had fallen on his back with the vampire hissing and smoking as it randomly touched the silver collar, while it tried to bite through the helmet and slash its black talons at inhumanly quick speed through the Kevlar armour.

Taro, went preternaturally calm. Even if the physical attacks were battering him and the fall backward had hurt his bruised back, he felt he could not raise the shotgun to any useful position. The Colt Dragoon was a better bet, so he let the shotgun fall away from his hand and reached for the handle of the pistol but the clawed foot of the vampire on top of him kept raking his arm away from it, while at the same time buffeting him with rapid attacks of both claws and inhumanly quick attempts to bite through his helmet. Taro gave up on reaching the pistol, and instead swung his arm out to the side, at ninety degree to his body, then swung it in as hard as possible in the general area above his chest. He hit something that felt both relatively light, yet also solid. Like a bird with a steel skeleton. At any rate it moved the vampire enough that he managed to reach the knife handle on his chest and unclip it. Then he swung his left arm out to the side and up above and then back towards him. He trapped the Vampire momentarily against his own body. And even though the creature was a lot stronger than Taro, it was not very voluminous, their bodies tended to the anorexically thin, so Taro had managed to wrap his arm around the creature and also grab onto his own webbing on the uniform. The vampire didn't even try to get out of his one-armed bear hug at first. Instead it just tried to push its talons into his throat despite the silver band burning it and making it hiss in rage and pain. But while Taro felt the attempt at his neck and it scared him, he also drew the right hand, back, knife in hand, and then, as fast as he could he started stabbing the vampire from the side and top, not carrying if he hit his own armour with each strike as it bit deeply into the abomination above him. The screeches intensified as did the hissing and the vampire now tried to shove away from Taro, but Taro held on to his own webbing and kept the creature trapped, though it somehow lifted Taro's weight enough to almost have Taro roll on top of it. Taro didn't stop stabbing it. And the creature now went from trying to slash and bite him to trying to free itself. It was all happening very fast, and Taro was not processing things consciously, only with his body, as years of training kicked in and he sensed the creature was about to get away, sliding up past him. He stabbed down on himself, feeling the tip of the knife bite a little into his armour as the knife slammed through the vampire's upper body and pinned it against Taro.

The thing went practically insane, shifting and raging so fast Taro lost the grip on his webbing with the left hand as he was buffeted all over the floor by the vampire that had now taken on a clearly demonic level of speed, hypersonic screeching and hissing, and chaotic movement all at once. Yet it remained pinned against Taro by the knife which it could not reach with its talons.

Taro was dimly aware of other men in the room, some gunfire, then suddenly he was engulfed in flame, and the vampire above him screeched even louder but began to flail more and more weakly. Eventually it stopped, but Taro was getting hot and started to worry. He stood, not removing his knife yet; and when he did, part of the flames, but not all of them fell away from him too. Strangely, vampires turned to dust if you shot them with Holy-water filled silver or if direct sunlight hit them on the exposed skin long enough, but apparently, if you burned them with a flamethrower they merely decomposed to burned skeletons.

Taro still had flames on him and he then felt people patting him down. One of the men took one of the cowls of the vampires and eventually they switched the fire still on Taro off. Ciasco had flamed him up to get rid of the vampire as shooting it when it was moving that fast and at such close range could have meant hitting Taro, and the suits were essentially fireproof. Not that Taro had known it.

He thanked the men, who had dispatched the other two vampires by shooting them as soon as they had been kicked off the men they had attacked. Taro being odd man out and not part of the team was the last to have been attended to and by then he had grappled the vampire to his own body, meaning kicking it away was not really an option.

After they regrouped, they investigated what was behind the door. It was a long corridor lined with barred doors. Twenty in all. Six of the cells had dead children in them, and five held barely living ones. Ciasco radioed for the Americans, who, to their credit, airlifted the children out after putting them on IVs and checking their pulse and basic life-signs. They had been starved and beaten. And probably worse.

They found no one else, nor any documents in the villa, and the hard drives in the server rooms were all gone too. Ciasco made sure a fire department truck was all hooked up first, then he used his flame-thrower to set fire to the entire building. The firemen would see the blaze did not extend to the nearby properties, and Ciasco made a call to a local construction firm. Got the owner to come to the site as the blaze was going and Taro heard Ciasco telling the man that the building must be razed to the ground and the rubble left there once the fire was out. Ciasco signed some papers that he gave the man. In the meantime, he had ordered his four guys to go door to door and question everyone in a two-block radius.

By the time they returned to base it was evening. Taro was exhausted. The armour was not light and it didn't breathe very well. When he removed it back at the base, he'd left puddles of sweat on the floor. As had the other men. Before they headed to the showers, Taro took the knife back to Marco. Marco took the knife, but held it without moving. He just looked at Taro, then asked him to turn around. Taro did while keeping an eye on Marco.

"Tagged you good," said Marco, poking at the large purple welt the size of a small fist on Taro's left side high on the lower back with the sheath of the knife. Taro winched a little and shifted a bit but didn't say anything.

"Rib ok? Broken?"

"Don't know. Cracked maybe. Doubt it's broken-broken."

"You gonna work with us again old man?"

"I don't know, unwise young man."

Marco laughed.

"Tell you what. I'll hold onto the knife, but if we work together again you come remind me to let you use it, okay?"

"Sure. Thanks. You wanna tell me about your brother?"

Marco just looked at Taro. Showed nothing in his eyes. *Granite face,* thought Taro, *just like the other guys in this unit.*

"He was older than me. Died. Bunch of orcs got him. There was a horde of them on the outskirts of the city, don't know if you heard. Hundreds of the fuckers."

Taro shook his head. He had not known of anything beyond his own little area near Monte Castello. He had never even seen an orc. Much less a horde, but thanks to Cooper's Compendium, he knew they tended to appear in groups.

Marco shook his head, but didn't look away from Taro.

"I couldn't get to him. I had a dozen or so on me too. I managed to get rid of them eventually, but it was too late. They had managed to get his helmet off. They had broken his head with axes and pieces of steel reinforcing bars. I did get all of them though. He'd not even managed to fire his Beretta. Mine was empty. I got to his by… I don't know, I just went crazy. Stabbing, punching, then I had his 93, and I fired. A few tried to run, but I reloaded and fired and chased them down. The last one I stabbed maybe a hundred times." Marco paused, then added, "Didn't bring him back."

"I'm sorry. What was his name?"

"Luca."

Taro crossed himself. "May he rest in peace."

Marco nodded, then said a simple "Thanks."

15

The unexpected good news came a full day later. The Americans has set up road blocks and one of them had stopped and captured Samuele Schwartz and two of his henchmen, colleagues, lovers, or whatever they may have been.

Douglas had only just heard the news in the late evening and had shared it with Taro just before both families retired for the night. The Valenti home was being reinforced and would not be usable for at least a week or two, so they were being hosted by Douglas and his wife Kate. The kids loved it, being a new adventure and having other little friends to play with, but Taro was uncomfortable in anyone else's home other than his own.

Taro had asked if they could go to the base to help with the questioning. Douglas just shook his head.

"Tomorrow. Tomorrow we go in together and we get debriefed too. Tonight sleep. And rest. You need it old man."

That's twice, thought Taro, thinking about the old joke of the wealthy man with the limousine driver and the trophy wife. *Twice I been called old man in one day. Uppity fuckers. I have half a mind to go full educational on the next younger asshole that takes the liberty. Stiff shoulder, back and possibly bust rib permitting, of course.* He often had such an internal dialogue to amuse himself with when circumstances didn't permit him to voice his thoughts. Despite what Jane always said, Taro wasn't without manners or etiquette. He wouldn't tell Douglas to go fuck himself in front of his lady of a wife.

When he got to bed Jane noticed he was moving stiffly and then had quickly forced Taro to turn and show the bruise. She gasped. It looked swollen, and really ugly. Taro told her it was fine and he'd be okay in a couple of days but she told him that she was getting the village doctor to take a look tomorrow. Taro was too tired to argue, so he agreed. But not if it got in the way of questioning that Freemason the Americans had captured. He didn't tell her why, other than he was exhausted, but he went to sleep rather quickly because he figured if he got a chance to have a few minutes alone with this Samuele, he wanted to be as physically capable of destroying the man without killing him as quickly as possible. With his bare hands, because he already knew they wouldn't let him near the guy with a weapon on him.

In the morning Jane won out, because Douglas told Taro their visit to the base was scheduled for the afternoon. The doctor had put some kinaesthetic tape on Taro after spreading a gel over the bruise that would help with the contusion. An X-ray machine was not available in the village but one could be remedied in Rimini. The doctor filled out a prescription sheet for it, which Taro was amused by. The simple bureaucratic process of needing a doctor's note for an X-ray amused him, given what had transpired over the last few years. It somehow put him in a better mood, which was definitely a first in his life.

*Bureaucracy giving me serenity. Shit, maybe I **am** getting senile!*

He spent the morning being pleasant and happy with Jane and the children. Going over some math problems for Marco and Arianna's homework, and teaching Alina how to load a revolver, even though he only let her fire it at a target with him helping and showing her how. Jane was there too for once, using Douglas' private range to practice a bit herself and check on the progress the kids were making. Taro was in charge of Arianna and Alina, the others being old enough to be safe on their own by now.

When they were ready to go in for lunch Taro looked at his wife and she looked back at the little group of their children, from the teenage girls, Anna taller than Jane now, and pretty, all the way to blonde little Alina and her serious and detailed demeanour.

They smiled at each other. It wasn't exactly a day at the beach, but it would do. Life was still good. He put his arm around her shoulders and she held his waist carefully because of his bruise, walking back together, and at peace.

Taro idly wondered about the seaside, and if there were really big monsters in the sea now. And what kind of boat would be safe to hunt them in, or at least not get eaten by them in. He had always liked catamarans. A really big catamaran would do it. One made of steel. *Yeah. I wonder if I could find a way to get one made. And... harpoon or machine gun at the front? Duh! Both. Obviously. I really must be getting old if I had to wonder at that!*

Jane was thinking that if the world was not so terribly unsafe, she was barely just young enough she might be able to make one more baby with Taro. *I mean, the world is absolutely insane now. Making more babies is the only thing that makes any sense to me anymore. The most sense. The only sense, really. And it was probably always that way.*

General Vaude, had not forgotten Taro's slight, though outwardly he didn't show it. He had simply limited himself to saying that civilians could not be part of the debriefing. Douglas had pointed out he was a civilian too, but Vaude had simply corrected himself that civilians who were not contracted to the military could not attend. General Aviliani had politely indicated that Taro Valenti actually was now a subcontracted civilian adviser to the *Gruppo d'Intervento Speciale - Carabinieri*, or GIS as they were usually referred to. He had also made it up on the spot, because although he was older, he had not lost his sense of shit-stirring here and there for his own amusement. One had to find life's little pleasures where one could, after all.

"Contracted to the US military!" Had said Vaude stiffly.

Aviliani had made a face. An exasperated face, spread his hands, huffed a bit, made a show of it, then spoke calmly in his accented English but with that real sense of concern on his face.

"General Vaude, in these times, surely, you know how much we need to co-operate with all useful parties. This man, Valenti, yes, he was unforgivably rude the other day. Unforgivably, no question," Aviliani was looking at the table now, shaking his head, ashamed, clearly ashamed of his countryman's deep faux-pas. "I understand completely General. In my youth, such a man would have been brought up on serious charges. *Serious charges!*" He was wagging his finger now, looking general Vaude directly in the eye.

"But... these are dangerous times, and in fairness to the man, he was put through his paces by my team for his insubordination, I assure you. You will see it on his face. Not to mention his body. Oh yes. They had a few words with him General, you will see. We may need him, but he's been taught a proper lesson in etiquette General, you can be sure of it. And his information and his dedication to the fight against the Satanists and all their creatures cannot be questioned General. Cannot be questioned." Aviliani was shaking his head now, with his lips pushed out, an expression of utter certainty on his half-closed eyes, as if the mere act of doubting was an imponderable sin.

"That man single-handedly figured out most of what we know today about how to defeat these demonic things. The thing is, General, we need his mind."

Vaude was not a stupid man, though he was vain. *The old bastard was badly cast as a General.* He thought. *He should have been a theatre actor. Then again, every fucking Italian was a good actor, was it not Orson Wells who had said that? That the only bad Italian actors are the ones that worked in film?* Yeah, he was sure it was Orson Wells.

"Very well. Show him in then."

Taro had been made to wait outside the meeting room, and as he entered now, Vaude was surprised to see the man actually had some bruises on his face. No one had mentioned that Taro had been on the raid of the Freemason Temple and that the bruising had come from the frenetic wrestling with a vampire.

Taro for his part, entered the large room quietly and sat in one of the chairs without saying a word.

"Right then. We can start now," said Vaude.

"Samuele Schwartz has identified several men as the architects of the opening of the portals. Or at least, as far as he is able to determine, their code names. Whether they are merely another step in the hierarchy remains to be seen, but at any rate, he is aware that there are six of these men, and he knows their code names. They are as follows," he then listed them out one by one.

"Prince Abeleth: North America;

Prince Orath: Asia;

Prince Rathienor: Australia;

Prince Kaarik: South America;

Prince Jakkiry: Africa;

Prince Laduvim: Europe;"

"Apparently there is also another group, which he is unsure if they are human or other, that are in control in Antarctica, which he has never dealt with directly or seen, and that are known simply as *The Watchers*. Certain Biblical passages have been interpreted as these being the demons of Hell, including Satan, as having been imprisoned there, and the events of the last few years possibly being the End of Days. That at least, seems to be a belief also shared by Mr. Schwartz; with a twist. The "Princes" And the "Barons" which he fancies himself as being one of, will be ruling the remaining survivors of humanity, bringing in a new age of plenty. At least for him and his masters anyway."

General Aviliani took over speaking in his accented English at a sign from General Vaude.

"Schwartz was not completely sure of the exact location of these "Princes" but he gave several locations he thought each might reside at. More importantly, he provided a location he believed they meet at for important meetings, as well as a day he though they would be there. He came to this conclusion based on the fact that he was to receive further notifications nine days from now. He also noted there was usually a three-day delay between notifications he received and events actually having happened earlier. So, he expects that maybe five or at most six days from now they would be meeting at what he believes is the pre-eminent refuge for them in Switzerland. We are currently putting together a team from Northern Italy of about 50 men, with support from Russian forces en-route. The idea is to have forward observers keep an eye on it, which is what the Russians will be doing as of later today or tomorrow, and then our guys go in once we know at least some, or even all, of these bastards are in there."

When Aviliani finished speaking there was complete silence in the room. After a few seconds, General Aviliani asked: "Questions?"

Taro put his hand up a bit. Aviliani had told him to behave himself if he was allowed back in the room prior to the meeting, so he was hesitant to just speak out. Aviliani nodded at him even as Vaude made a face that barely concealed distaste or irritation.

"The fifty guys going into this place... I assume it's an underground bunker, they are from a single unit or are they a multi-national force?" asked Taro neutrally.

Aviliani nodded a little before responding.

"They are all from a surviving battalion of Italian Alpine forces. They are all volunteers and have their own choice of weapons. We will be shipping as many of the armours as we have that they may need, and anything else they ask for that we have."

Taro asked one more question, this time without raising his hand or asking permission in any way.

"Do they have a priest with them? A battle priest?"

"A... battle priest?" Asked Vaude. He was a Baptist originally and while he accepted that only original Catholic sacraments seemed to have any effects on the Hellspawned, he still had not officially converted to Catholicism. In his mind it was still a Pagan-influenced perversion of *real* Christianity. And the pomposity of the Papists irritated him no end.

"Yes Sir," replied Taro, forcing himself to say the *Sir* without grinding his teeth, or clenching his jaw.

"A priest can hold a lot of the creatures we have dealt with over the years at bay. And can even detect them at a distance in certain cases. It would be a most useful addition for the soldiers involved."

"Hmm. I'll let the commander in charge know." And it was clear from his demeanour that Vaude would not be pleased to entertain any further questions from Taro.

The only other announcement was that there were no active portals open anywhere on the planet now, and that Russian and German forces were trying to co-ordinate a take-over of the entire CERN facility, though this was a difficult operation since everyone wanted to capture the super-collider intact, and the CERN laboratories had massive co-ordinated private armies even three years ago, and now there were initial reports of the CERN army containing supernatural elements too. There had even been unconfirmed reports of dragon-riders and giants flinging some horrific, flying porcupine type of creatures, that deployed as crunched up balls similar to hedgehogs, and then would suddenly spread their balled up wings over their enemies, before launching hundreds of deadly poisonous spikes that would penetrate Kevlar armour unless it encountered ceramic plates.

Taro wanted very badly to ask why they would not just nuke the entire CERN area, but he already knew the answer. All these bastards, whoever they were, wanted to have the control of CERN. They all wanted access to that demonic technology that opened portals to Hell.

Taro started to imagine how one might get a huge nuclear device close enough anyway. The meeting was ended while he was still trying to calculate the fuel and load requirements that a helicopter or plane would need to get close enough.

Taro and Douglas were free to return to their homes, and Taro planned to follow the works at his home, to make sure the reinforcements were done properly, then he thought he just wanted to get in his home with his family and shut the rest of the world and its hellish minions out. Including the ones that never came through a portal but were always on this side already; and created CERN to begin with.

16

De Dominicis had received some very cool Kevlar armour with ceramic plates in it, big red crosses on the chest, silver collars to protect the neck, built-in radios in the helmets, which also had IR and night-vision and the ability to switch modes integral to their design.

His men had all been fitted out with these armours and every weapon they had asked for had been provided. Including one he had guessed at might exist but really wasn't sure, and yet, here he had it in his hand. A three-kilo weight, in the shape of a more rounded Rugby ball. Pure white with a small digital display on it that currently spelt INACTIVE in red letters. It could be activated and have a timer set for anything between one and thirty minutes. It could also be detonated instantly by bypassing two security codes and entering a final suicidal code. He had no idea how the thing worked, or if it even was nuclear —strictly speaking— but he had been told that he should not have any friendlies within at least 600 metres and preferably at least a kilometre. Even then the radiation would likely kill you after some months or a few years, so he assumed it was indeed nuclear. Though how they got it to be so small he couldn't understand. He had been given five of these things, and he had given one to each of the five groups of ten men he had subdivided his team into. They had selected and promoted four more Sergeants, one for each ten-man group, and eight more corporals, so that each team could be split into two teams of five, one led by the sergeant and one by one of the corporals, the other corporal being a spare in case one of the other officers died.

De Dominicis had Tiramino and D'Amaso in his own ten-man group, though he was also the overall leader of the mission, and he had a further two corporals already in his team.

They were due to ship out tomorrow and had had very little time to train and co-ordinate with each other, but he had managed to get a local seamstress to make patches for all his men.

It was a small thing, but each man now had his name on a strip of material stitched to their armour's exterior Kevlar, and a patch on the left shoulder with the words Black Company at the top and Nec Spe Nec Metu at the bottom. They had dropped the word "Luck" by unanimous decision. For a logo they had selected a flared red cross with crossed swords over it.

Russian and German troops were already engaging the CERN Army since yesterday, and De Dominicis hoped this would distract people enough from their own arrival. They were going in on a dozen helicopters, but half of them were just carrying fuel for the second leg of the trip, as they would need to stop half-way to refuel to give the pilots enough fuel to drop off the team and get back close enough to the Italian border to be refuelled again in preparation for the extraction.

The Black Company would be dropped about five to ten kilometres away from the underground facility that had been identified by Russian spotters as containing the leaders of the Satanic sect that had caused the death of well over half the planet's population and the current infestation of Hellspawn still raging across the Earth.

De Dominicis had no illusions about this being a mission that would be easy or even succeed at all, but he truly hoped, and prayed fervently before lying down to sleep, that they would kill the evil bastards involved.

He managed to sleep well and be fully rested for the first time in months.

17

Taro's home had been fixed and all the windows and entrances reinforced massively. He had taken time with his wife and children, even if the influx of Hellspawned creatures had ramped up, but Monte Castello was one of the better defended villages and everyone did their part manning the village walls or the equivalent, which for the Valenti was their border wall.

They had faced a relatively small horde of orcs, which looked exactly as most people imagined them from seeing the film The Lord of the Rings. This convinced Taro that his idea that these creatures may originate from a plane that gave form to the imaginings of the inhabitants of our plane of existence, had merit.

He had been on one section of the wall with Marco, and they had both fired their rifles quickly and efficiently. Marco being faster than his father due to the SFAR being a semi-automatic rifle, while Taro's RPR was a bolt action. Marco had accounted for twelve orcs and Taro ten, and the boy had been so proud of having outdone his dad that he told everyone he knew. In what he thought was a modest way, of course, but it fooled no one. He loved his father but was ecstatic he had finally done something better than him. Taro for his part smiled and let the boy have his victory; it was well-deserved.

Arianna of course now wanted to shoot orcs too and became a more regular addition to the shooting practices and also the manning of the wall. She had managed to shoot some Hellpig creature that looked like a mixture between a boar, a warthog and a wolf, and was about the size of small pony. It also had a ridiculous curly tail and six hooved legs. They had only seen one of the things, so Arianna was happy her kill was a unique creature. After ensuring it was safe, she had made a necklace with the larger tusks and a bracelet with the smaller ones, thanks to Anna's help. She wore the necklace for a while or when she went with Marco and Taro to the wall, calling it her Arianna Danger necklace. She had gifted the bracelet to Anna for helping her. Anna being too polite to tell her she didn't really want to wear a bracelet made from two curved, demon-pig tusks, had offered it to Scarlet instead, who loved it and wore it everywhere, making sure she told everyone it was a unique demon-pig-tusk bracelet. She didn't really notice how most children her age smiled worriedly and never talked about it much, despite Scarlet's enthusiasm for recounting the story of how her sister Arianna had shot the demon-pig.

Jane had supervised the extended precautions against ghosts and various other creatures as Cooper updated her daily on any new discoveries. She had placed automated sprayers, and nebulizers in every room of the house, as well as high up on the outside walls, and loaded them all with holy water that had Frankincense bubbled through it. She was planning on getting sprinklers with a closed system cistern to cover the grounds. Taro had shaken his head at the cost and expense that would entail, but she had given him a look, and he'd raised his hands in surrender and didn't mention it again; though he was noticing the dwindling pile of silver and smaller pile of gold they had left.

Three more giants had attacked the village outskirts, but had been dispatched relatively easily. Taro had shot one and Douglas another, both had used the .50 calibre sniper rifles they had been "gifted" or rather, had never-returned to the Rimini base. The last giant had been injured by one of Alessandro's traps and the town people toyed with the idea of hunting it down and trying to capture it alive. Taro had intended to go after it and kill it, but he had been beaten to it by a family of farmers that had somehow survived relatively far from the village without even having taken all that many precautions. They had miraculously not lost anyone, though their home had been damaged, and they were glad to be accepted into the village. A roughly equivalent spot of farmland to theirs had been allocated to them too. The giant had had one of those pouches with ten of those gold plates, so they were able to afford to pay for it all and still had five plates left over.

On the day the assault on the underground base in far-off Switzerland, where the leading Satanists were thought to be, had begun, Douglas had come to visit Taro. He had a small suitcase made of wood with him. He'd asked Taro if they could go talk in the workshop, away from any digital devices.

They were now sitting across from each other, the wooden suitcase on a workbench nearby, two glasses between them, and a rare and expensive bottle of tequila between them. They clinked glasses and downed a shot each, then Douglas spoke first.

"So, they are trying to keep CERN active even if they get control of it."

"Yeah. I know," replied Taro, reaching for the square bottle of Herradura Tequila, and pouring them another shot.

Douglas didn't reach for the glass, and neither did Taro.

"Could we nuke it?" asked Taro casually. Douglas sniffed, amused, then reached for the glass and looked up at Taro and realised the other man wasn't joking. He stopped. Glass half-way to his mouth.

His brain started spinning. Taro could see the man trying to calculate a bunch of things. He'd started to set the glass down.

Taro hadn't touched his.

"Yes!" replied Douglas almost excited.

"Yes, I think we can!"

Taro made an impressed face and nodded, while making a slight winding motion with his left hand, intending for Douglas to continue.

"I can request enough uranium to study the frequencies of the creatures... did I tell you? We captured another Hellfrog. Second one I have seen ever. I hope there isn't more of them, they are so deadly... anyway, the thing is, I have been getting Cooper, and his fiancé Lea, to start studying the EM frequencies, and the rad counts… and…" Taro was wind-milling his hand faster, "yeah, ok, anyway, the thing is I can request uranium for the tests. A bunch of uranium. And other stuff too. Explosives, certainly. A bunch of stuff. Yes. We could build one. I mean, I could. Or maybe here. In your workshop…"

Taro squinted. "I have my gun guy here most days, he's supposed to start on the other Colt Dragoon…"

"Yeah, about that. I don't think you'll need it. Remember how about a year ago you told me you had a fantasy gun idea you liked? From a computer game I think, a character called Rico. Anyway, I remember the picture you had showed me that someone had made of it." As he was talking Douglas had moved the tequila glass carefully out of the way and reached for the wooden case, and laid it down flat on the workbench. He was now popping the clasp on it.

Taro began to almost have his brain freeze. *He couldn't have… it's not possible…*

Douglas swung the suitcase around and said: "Open it."

Taro looked at Douglas, his mouth opened a little but he didn't say anything. Then he looked at the case and pushed the lid up.

And there it was. A thing of beauty. Stainless Steel. White ivory handle inserts. And a ramped style front sight with barely adjustable rear sights so they would not be bulky and snag, and Douglas had even got the delicate motif right: a plant stalk with leaves ending in a small, golden, bell-shaped flower near the end of the barrel. But most amazing of all was the under-barrel integrated launcher. Taro was not sure what it fired, but he was pretty sure that Douglas being the kind of guy he was, this thing was as accurate as the original fantasy design.

"This… it fires…"

Douglas nodded. "Yup. Smallish but potent frag grenades, or smoke signals, or dragon-breath rounds. I got you six of each type in the car along with the holster and belt to go with it."

"This is… I don't know what to say, it's beautiful Doug. I really… yeah… I am not going to say you shouldn't have, because you definitely should have, but I am not sure why you did this. Or how."

Douglas laughed. He had never seen Taro at a loss for words before.

"Well, I figured you deserved it a long while ago, and the recent event that made you give me a warning before that freak with the six vampires came to my place and I had to deal with them the way you did, well… it was already done by then, but it convinced me I had done the right thing by getting it made for you."

"But how?" Taro was still shocked, and looking at the gun in its case which was somewhat garishly lined in red velvet. It contrasted nicely with the white ivory and the golden flower though. *A bit pimp,* thought Taro, *but man, I am **not** complaining!*

"I do have quite a bit of pull in the USA too you know. And I just said I wanted it made to the exact specs I sent them."

"So, this is…"

"Yup. It's chambered in .454 Casull. Six rounds. And it weighs a ton. It will probably put your hip and your back out and you'll need an anvil on the left side to counter balance it. Then you'll probably lose an inch as your spine is compressed."

Taro picked up the handgun finally. He opened the revolver's drum and checked it was empty. Then took out the box of shells that was also in its place in the case, took out six shells and loaded it, then closed it. It was indeed heavy.

"I think I want the rest of it, Doug. And… thank you. This is without a doubt the best present I ever had. Or am likely to ever get."

Well, what do you know, the ornery old bastard does have a heart after all, and all it took was several thousand dollars or precision machined steel and explosive death made to order to make him gush. Thought Douglas, smiling.

After Taro had put on the leather holster and belt, he had loaded the belt. It had space for six of the grenades, and twelve of the .454 Casull rounds. For the grenades he picked one smoke, three fragmentation and two dragon-breaths. He spent the next half an hour showing it off to his wife and children. Marco wanted one too, until Taro told him when he was bigger he'd give him the Colt Dragoon, but right now even that gun was too heavy for him, and this one certainly was.

"What are you going to call it daddy?" It was Alina, her innocent blue eyes and blonde hair so intent in her little face. It just came to him spontaneously: "How about I call it Alina, just like you?"

She thought about it for a while, then said, "But that's my name. I am Alina. That is a gun," then she brightened up and added, "Alina-gun. That is the Alina gun. Because it has a flower."

Arianna and Scarlet of course now also wanted guns named after them and only Anna, catching her father's eye above the heads of her younger siblings, pointed to herself and shook her head silently while making a slightly horrified face. She didn't want any guns named after her.

"Girls! That's silly. That gun can be named after Alina because it's the only one like that. Right dad?" Marco, glanced at his father quickly, who nodded, so he continued, "Every other gun already has a name. Like dad's other gun is a Colt Dragoon. In .44 magnum. And the other gun is a Colt 1911, or the Ruger Magnum .357 revolver, they all have names. And a gun called Scarlet or Arianna would be silly. They are silly names for a gun."

"Well, Alina is also a silly name for a gun!" Said Scarlet, "It's a girl's name for a gun! That makes no sense!" Ever the family lawyer, if she wasn't going to have a gun named after her, neither should anyone else. *So, there!*

"It's not a silly name," said Marco slightly enraged. He and Alina seemed to have a deeper connection than he had with his other sisters. She was definitely his favourite anyway, as both his parents knew.

"It has a *flower!*" He pointed at the engraving on the gun while he raised his voice. Taro had started to give the dad look to the whole room, so Scarlet just shook her head and wandered off muttering under her breath.

The room went quiet, Douglas amused at the chaos Taro's children invariably seemed to cause at the drop of a hat. And always in such absurd ways. His own kids were more normal. *Thank God!* he thought.

"Okay daddy, you can call your gun Alina. It's the Alina gun." Alina was smiling happily and had her hands together after making a few excited applauses, her blue eyes filled with joy while looking up at her father.

"Okay then. It's the Alina gun now," said Taro smiling back at her while he knelt down and gave his daughter a one-armed hug and a kiss on the top of her head.

"Can I shoot it daddy?" asked the little girl.

Taro thought about it for a half-second, before replying.

"The problem is this gun is *really* powerful and when you shoot it, it kicks very hard, even for me. But you can come see the first time I shoot it, okay?"

And now it was a family affair. All of them got their ear protection, including Jane and Douglas, and made the trip to the wall where a target was quickly set up. Taro cocked the handgun, took aim one handed, with a duelling style stance, and squeezed the trigger. The gun kicked a half foot high from its original point of aim, and the shock wave it caused in the air was physically felt by all.

Not as bad as I thought, thought Taro, pleased that the recoil was heavy but manageable. As the ammunition for it was limited, he did not take any more shots, but he was very pleased with it.

"It's like a small cannon, dad!" said Marco.

"Yes son, it is."

"Dad, when I am bigger, like you, can I shoot it too?"

"Yes. When you're a bit bigger."

"But… dad… like… how big? Like Anna, or just like mom?"

Taro laughed. "Yeah, maybe like mom-sized. When you get tall like her."

He looked at Jane and offered the pistol.

"Wanna try?"

Jane shook her head no.

"Come on…" said Taro wanting her to experience it.

"No, I'm scared I'll drop it! Then you'd probably shoot me with it!"

"Oh honey, I wouldn't do that! The ammo is rare and expensive. And it's heavy enough I could just pistol whip you with it, I mean, if you dropped it, it would be dirty already anyway."

Jane made a face. "Right! Think I'll just settle for the daily beating instead, darling!"

"Aw, come on, come here, I'll help you, you won't drop it. I'll hold it with you."

Eventually she relented and with Taro holding his hand over her own grip on the pistol, she did shoot it, hitting the target square on too.

"Whoa," she said, handing the gun back to Taro.

"That's not a gun I can use comfortably. Or at all really."

"It is heavy, and a bit much, but I think this could take down a giant." Taro was admiring the gun as he held it and started to reload the two fired rounds. He finished with: "I love it."

"I love it too dad," said Marco.

Jane shook her head, looking at Taro and Marco, smiling. *Men and boys. Such simple creatures to make happy, really.*

৵•৶

After lunch Douglas and Taro returned to the workshop and begun to make a list of components that they would need to make a portable nuclear bomb. They wrote things in a simple code, and had no digital devices anywhere near them. As they finished for the day, they both reflected on what an absurd position they were now finding themselves.

"You know, I probably can't make this thing in any way *clean,*" said Douglas emphasising the last word with air-quotes.

Taro nodded, before replying pensively, "well, maybe that's best, if it keeps everyone away from the site for a few millennia afterwards."

"Doubt it. Look at Chernobyl. People go there for fun." Douglas was not looking happy.

"Yeah but they don't live or work there anymore, and that's the idea."

"Sure, but it's also likely if we do this, we kill a whole bunch of innocents that live near there."

Taro did the math in his head but decided against stating the obvious. He knew Douglas felt guilty about the portals as a whole to begin with. So he took another approach.

"We don't know that, and anyway, there is going to be some fighting there right now. Any sensible civilian will have left that whole area."

"Maybe," replied Douglas dejectedly.

"Not maybe; for sure. Even if there are going to be any people there it would be the kind that would use that infernal thing again to do nothing good with it."

"Or soldiers…" said Douglas.

"Right. Just good guys following the orders of their Satanic masters, right? Come on Douglas, no one anywhere near CERN is innocent. Literally no one. And anyway, let's burn that bridge once we cross it."

"Don't you mean cross that bridge when we get to it?"

"Nope. I mean exactly what I said."

"Right… no going backwards eh?"

"I sure never have."

"Yeah. I can see that. You're a very special man Taro. Very special. We should really study your brain one day; just to check if it's because it's the size of a walnut, or because it's made of very hard volcanic rock that you have these unique powers!"

"Ha-ha Doug. But you know I'm right. These fuckers need to be taken out, and so does their portal creation machine."

Douglas looked at the floor a second or two before responding.

"I still don't have to like it."

"No one likes it Doug. No one is happy about it. But it just needs doing."

"Yeah. I know. And we will."

Taro nodded, and Douglas got up, ready to leave now.

"Look at the bright side, as a kid you probably would have loved the idea of building an atom bomb to crush bad guys. You're living the dream Douglas Jones!"

"Yeah. Pity it's mostly a fucking nightmare."

"Ehhh… what do you want, your life to be a chick-flick?"

"Well…"

"Don't. Don't you dare Doug. Not you too! Manly adventure films! With heroic protagonists winning against all odds. That's the films you like Douglas. Say it with me! Jason and the Argonauts kind of stuff. The Odyssey! Don't you go all metrosexual on me now Doug. I don't want a pink cloud when that thermonuclear thing goes off and kills all the bad guys."

"Orange. I think mostly it will be orange. Sorry. Not the fiery red of Hell you aspire to, I'm afraid."

"Red? No, no, Doug, I was going for pure white. The cleansing glow of justice."

"To be fair, it may be that, at the very start. You will probably go blind if you see it though."

"I don't need to see it Doug. I have faith. In you and your atomic prowess." He patted Douglas on the back as they stepped out of the workshop.

Epilogue

The six Princes of Hell were gathered in their communal throne room. Each held a black orb in their left hand and held it at the tip of each point of the six-pointed star etched in gold on the round table that they had recently added to the room. The original golden, six-pointed star was also present under the table, carved into the obsidian floor. Two vampires and a lich were in some kind of trance, swinging slightly back and forth, behind each of the old men.

"They have penetrated down to the deepest layers, Prince Abeleth. Are we still safe here?" It was Prince Rathienor, the Australian who had asked.

"Clearly, we are not completely safe, otherwise we would not be here with our servants behind us, would we?" Prince Abeleth was the eldest but his voice was firm with irritation for once.

"Do we have alternative exits?" asked Prince Jakkiry of Africa, despite his translucent skin. No people of colour could ever aspire to this level of power. The homosexual Obama had been as high as anyone of that sort had got, and it was several degrees and levels below the real power mongers, much less the apex of it as was present in this room.

"No." Lied Prince Abeleth smoothly.

Prince Laduvim noted the lie and resolved to become Abeleth's shadow. Even kill him, if necessary. There was bound to be at least one or two alternatives out of here, he thought. And if things turned bad, Abeleth would know what they were.

"Then we make our stand here. There aren't that many of them left, surely?" Prince Kaarik of South America was not even eighty years old, making him the impetuous youth he was from the perspective of the others.

"Indeed." Prince Abeleth lied smoothly again.

Prince Orath of Asia remained silent, but like Prince Laduvim, he resolved to stay close to Prince Abeleth no matter what happened.

"There seem to be only ten men left," said Prince Jakkiry, "surely our shades and liches will be enough to overpower them?"

"Perhaps," replied Prince Abeleth non-committedly.

ॐ•ॐ

De Dominicis was down to just nine men. They had fought for two days straight and lost almost half of their force just breaking into the underground city and clearing the first three levels.

They had managed to get a partial map of what was left and had methodically blocked off key corridors then sent patrols of four to six men to investigate and clear areas. In that way they had cleared the next six levels. There now appeared to be only one level left, for which they only had a partial map, but also an overall volume calculation which meant they knew that they had to clear approximately half the map area of the previous levels; assuming the various rooms and corridors retained the average height they had encountered so far.

De Dominicis was furious, sad and exhausted all at once. They had cleared all the upper floors for sure but he still ensured his men laid alarms: claymores against both human and supernatural enemies in five locations upstream and five downstream. Then he had split his force into two units of five in separate rooms, just in case. They were now safe in a ring of steel, blessed salt and holy water and three layers of claymore mines that would be deadly to anything alive or undead. He ordered his men to break out all the rations they had, cook, eat, drink and sleep. They had also found several stores of food and other gear, and they had beds in the rooms they had commandeered.

He may have only ten men left of The Black Company, and he could see that the men in it were hurt, damaged and tired, but none of them were broken. They knew what they were going after and they meant to finish it. The evil bastard that started all this, that were responsible for their family members dying, their friends in this assault dying, and so on. They were in here. They had separate multiple confirmations of it from the Russian recon team and also from their own data captures since they had been in the complex.

These self-styled Princes of Hell were about to come face to face with the wrath of what was left of The Black Company.

The men ate, they had found some excellent Cognac, Vodka and Tequila in one of the store rooms, and De Dominicis spoke to them earlier and told them that getting shit-faced was not an option, so they had to eat and eat well, and then they could take up to four shots each maximum. Three for their comrades in arms that had been lost, and one to whatever kept them going until they ended this.

The men obeyed. None were the kind to not be serious by this point. They ate well, drank their shots, then drank water and slept for the next ten hours with little interrupting them other than the nightmares they all had. When they woke, they had a light but slow breakfast, recovering their psychic wits and wiping off the mental cobwebs from the dreams. Among these last ten was also the Battle Priest. He offered a Holy Mass and communion to them all, then they made their prayers, checked and re-checked their vast assortment of weapons, buddied up in pairs, and then they set about recollecting the claymores blocking the path ahead. They left the ones blocking the way out in place after reconfiguring them. There was a very detailed and specific labyrinthine path to get through to defuse those. If none of them made it out of here, whatever killed them was unlikely to get out of here unscathed either.

It had been three days and Douglas had already received enough Uranium, C4, photon fuses, and other assorted equipment that he managed to get enough out of the base to begin building an atomic device in Taro's workshop. He'd just dropped off all the equipment and they could begin working on it in the evenings. Security at the military base in Rimini had been lax for Douglas because everyone knew him and everyone knew he was probably the man most responsible for the entire planet not having been completely overrun by Hellspawn. Yet, anyway.

Jane had come knocking on the workshop door, walkie talkie in hand. Taro had opened the door wondering what would prompt her to interrupt them, though they were essentially done for today.

"It's your brother. He's on the long-distance radio."

Taro ran out towards the main house, leaving Douglas to lock up.

Dario's voice was faint and crackly over the radio, but Taro recognised it clearly.

"I don't have much time. Not sure how long the connection will last, but we're on a boat. Going to try to make it through the Suez Canal into the med. Then up to you. What's the nearest port to you? Over."

"Rimini. If you get there, go to the US Army base there and tell them you are my brother, use our surname and tell them you are a friend of Douglas Jones too. Over."

"Okay. Who the fuck is Douglas Jones? Over."

"The guy who shut down all the portals to date. He's my friend. Over."

"Good to know. Okay, Taro, I have to go, we're still too close to shore and I… well, there are other people aboard besides us. I need to make sure everyone is… safe. Over."

Taro had understood the code and replied in kind.

"Okay, be careful and look after the boy and the wife. And don't be scared to throw any unnecessary weight and ballast overboard if you need to go faster. Lighter boats sail higher. Over."

"Yep. In hand. Hope to see you in a few weeks. Over and out."

"Godspeed brother. Over and out."

Their talk had been short, as was usual, and Taro was worried about whoever else was on that boat that Dario had to worry about. His brother didn't know anything about sailing, and in fairness, the little Taro knew was probably nowhere near enough to sail a boat from the Southern tip of Africa to Europe. *Still...* he thought, *I'd rather take my chances with storms and sea monsters than some dodgy fucks on the same boat as me and my child.* He prayed. It was all he could do, and he resolved to pray ten Hail Marys, a Pater Noster and a Gloria every day until he saw his brother again, or the unthinkable was confirmed to him somehow.

That evening, after he'd told Jane, and they were in bed, she hugged him, and they fell asleep that way, tired and worried, but hopeful.

The howling at the Moon that happened later in the night, in the distance, done by the leader of a small pack of werewolves a few kilometres away, did not wake them.

The End of In the Shadow of Monte Bianco

If you enjoyed this book and would like to read sequels to it, please let me know at my blog or by leaving me a good review at Amazon. I am an independent author and the only way for me to know what my readers enjoy is if they let me know.

Thank you.

ABOUT GIUSEPPE FILOTTO

WWW.GFILOTTO.COM

Giuseppe Filotto was born in Turin and grew up in Italy, Africa and England. He studied in Botswana, England and South Africa and is a qualified Civil Engineer and Clinical Hypnotist. He authored several novels and non-fiction books (see below).

He has worked in the construction industry for 30 years, being involved in the construction of several landmark buildings in London, England, and one in Astana, Kazakhstan. He is a life-long martial artist, having achieved a Second Dan in Shōtōkan Karate in 2001 in Cape Town, South Africa, where he also worked in armed close protection for several years. He later became a certified Systema Instructor (The Russian Martial System) by Mikhail Ryabko in Moscow, in February of 2008.

He has moved 54 times at age 54 as of 2024, and would now like to settle down and just write books; so, he wants you to know he is very grateful for your purchase.

He is married with five children, and is attempting to make his small —and difficult to maintain— Olive and Truffle farm produce some regular income.

So far, he's failing miserably at being a farmer and is looking forward to the impending Apocalyptic collapse, when his natural inclination towards being a Catholic Baron/Warlord, instead of a farmer, will, he feels, "shine through". He also thinks that given a little warning, werewolves and vampires would be more fun to deal with than the current crop of global politicians, judges and lawyers, that roam the Earth unchecked.

BOOKS BY GIUSEPPE FILOTTO

All my books in **paper format** are available on Amazon under
Giuseppe Filotto, G. Filotto, or Filotto

**All E-book Digital Editions are available directly at my digital
store https://payhip.com/EBOOKSBYGFILOTTO or
accessible from my blog at www.gfilotto.com. Some books are
only available in one or the other format.**

***

Listed in Chronological Order (newest books at the end)

***

The Face on Mars (1995 – updated in 2014) – Non-fiction. An investigation into the artificial objects in the Cydonia region, the destruction of Mars and the technologies related to them. A tour de-force of human history that has been plagiarised in part by Graham Hancock of Chariots of the Gods fame.

The Dirty Old West – (2010) – This is a Role Playing Game that uses a simplified version of the same Quick, Omni-Rolepalying Game (Q.O.R.G.) mechanics of the SCZA RPG Game (see above). It is set in a dusty and bloody version of the Wild West and can be used to have hours of Bounty Hunting, Bandit, Red Indian revenge fun with your friends, some six-sided dice and pen and paper.

Systema: The Russian Martial System (2011) – Non-Fiction. A demythologising and explanation of the methods and training of the Russian Martial art that took all martial artists by surprise starting in the mid 1990s. This was the first and to date remains the most complete manual on explaining how and why Systema can produce results that maze even experienced martial artists.

Overlords of Mars – Inception (Book 1 – 2011) – Fiction. A hidden world of antigravity machines, Nazi bases on the Moon and Allied forces on Mars that the average person on Earth is completely unaware of is introduced.

Overlords of Mars – Stasis (Book 2 – 2013) – Fiction. The continuation from book 1, set on Mars and the subterfuge, intrigue, lost history and space battles make for quite a cinematographic story line that would adapt well to film.

Confederate Rising – (2019) – Fiction. A stand alone adventure novella set in the far-future of the same universe as the Overlords of Mars series but an interlude before book 3 of that series comes out, hopefully sometime in 2019.

NAZI MOON - Overlords of Mars Ominbus of the first Trilogy including Book I - Inception, Book II - Stasis, and Book III - Black Sun (Books 1 to 3 – 2023) – Fiction. The continuation from book 1, and 2, explores in more depth the Nazi Regime on Luna in Book 3. With even more intrigue, lost history and Nazi advanced technology and mysticism. Book 3 will be released on its own sometime in 2024.

Believe! : Real Christianity Taking Christendom Back – A Reply to the Pederast Infested Vatican, the Churchians of All Denominations, and a Manual for Atheists, Agnostics and Would-be Pagans – (2019) – Non-fiction. With a title that is the marketing nightmare of publishers, this work was described by Daniel Eness, the Hugo Nominated author of the blog series *Safe Space as Rape Room* as follows:

I would say Filotto's Believe! Appears to take a "no prisoners" approach to the consideration of Christian faith, but it does quite the opposite. It takes the existing prisoners of a broad range of fundamentally corrupting passions in the eternal hope of freeing them.

His enemy is our Enemy, and it in Believe! That he charts his course, both personal and universal, for the retaking of Christendom. The unabashed nature in which the author takes on a host of errors, heresies and misunderstandings of and within the Christian faith will drive away many readers. Those who remain will become champions of the faith.

In Believe! Filotto exemplifies a unique and sorely-needed class of character that has as yet eluded the catalogues of role-playing games everywhere: The Theologian- Berserker.

Reclaiming The Catholic Church: The True History of Vatican II and the Visible Remnant of the Real Catholic Church now that the Vatican is a Pederast Infested Hive of Impostors – (2020) – At 530 pages, and pulling no punches this book, builds on the brief introduction to Catholicism expressed in BELIEVE! (see above) and details the differences between actual Catholicism and the Pagan, child-molesting, Freemasonic Vatican II produced, fake Novus Orco Church headed by non-Catholic Bergoglio. Provides details of the infiltration, the heresies in each Vatican II document, the Canon Law which expressly states every antipope from 28th October to today is not even Catholic, much less a Pope or a valid cleric of Catholicism, and most important of all, refutes every single argument made against Sedeprivationism in detail. A detailed structure of the objections as well as brutal examples of some of the objectors are described. BELIEVE! resulted in conversions to Catholicism and a return to it by "cradle Catholics" that were fooled into the Novus Orco sect. In this book, you get the details and the weapons, to fight back against the liars, deceivers and would be destroyers of Catholicism.

Surviving the Current ZOMBIE APOCALYPSE Using the new Q.O.R.G RPG System – (2022) – This is a complete pen and paper Role Playing Game using a system that only requires two six-sided dice and some friends to have hours of

entertaining, dramatic, horror-inspired fun. Using every Conspiracy Theory doing the rounds on the Internet, this work has been described as hilarious and being worth buy for just the reading entertainment value. Full colour interior.

Zombie Apocalypse: Inception – (2022) – The first module for the Surviving the Current Zombie Apocalypse (SCZA) RPG, places the players in a remote little village that is soon going to be overrun with... Zombie. Includes pre- generated characters and various possible storylines. Requires the Main Rules to be played.

Caveman Theory: How to win at Sex, Love and Relationships in the Current Zombie Apocalypse – (2024) - The Modern World wants you to be bitter, weak, miserable, and lonely. This book rejects that perspective and is about as politically incorrect as you will find, while not agreeing with PUAs, Red Pillers, MGTOW, or any of the various "Churchian" models of marriage, it presents empirically testable and observable realities in a direct manner. The intent within it is to lead men and women into positive, healthy relationships, demystifying the sexes to one another and getting rid of the lies that we have been taught about both. The ultimate aim being to be able to find that one relationship that can lead to a secure marriage that lasts a lifetime. While the book might be considered to be aimed mostly at men, it is a very useful tool for women too. The brutal truths about both men and women are identified within it, as are the strategies and knowledge to understand the underlying reasons for them and how to integrate them into a more wholesome and holistic approach to love, family and life in general.

***

You can keep up with Giuseppe at his blog: www.gfilotto.com

Viewer Discretion Advised

Or watch his videos on various topics at his YouTube channel: https://www.youtube.com/@The-Kurgan/videos

Remember: the wise readers never try to find out about the authors they like the writing of!